# The
# Ocean Within

*V. M. Caldwell*

*illustrated by Erica Magnus*

MILKWEED EDITIONS

© 1999, Text by V. M. Caldwell
© 1999, Cover painting and interior illustrations by Erica Magnus
All rights reserved. Except for brief quotations in critical articles or reviews, no part of this book may be reproduced in any manner without prior written permission from the publisher: Milkweed Editions, 430 First Avenue North, Minneapolis, MN 55401. (800) 520-6455. www.milkweed.org
Distributed by Publishers Group West

Published 1999 by Milkweed Editions
Printed in the United States of America
Cover painting and interior illustrations by Erica Magnus
Cover design by Gail Wallinga
Interior design by Elizabeth Cleveland
The text of this book is set in Electra.
99 00 01 02 03  5 4 3 2 1
*First Edition*

Milkweed Editions, a nonprofit publisher, gratefully acknowledges support from Alliance for Reading Funders: Silicon Graphics Inc.; Dayton Hudson Circle of Giving; Ecolab Foundation; Musser Fund; Jay and Rose Phillips Foundation; Target Stores; United Arts School and Partnership Funds; James R. Thorpe Foundation. Other support has been provided by Elmer L. and Eleanor J. Andersen Foundation; James Ford Bell Foundation; Bush Foundation; Dayton Hudson Foundation on behalf of Dayton's, Mervyn's California, and Target Stores; Doherty, Rumble & Butler Foundation; Gerneral Mills Foundation; Honeywell Foundation; McKnight Foundation; Minnesota State Arts Board through an appropriation by the Minnesota State Legislature; Norwest Foundation on behalf of Norwest Bank Minnesota; Lawrence and Elizabeth Ann O'Shaughnessy Charitable Income Trust in honor of Lawrence M. O'Shaughnessy; Oswald Family Foundation; Ritz Foundation on behalf of Mr. and Mrs. E. J. Phelps Jr.; John and Beverly Rollwagen Fund of the Minneapolis Foundation; St. Paul Companies, Inc.; Star Tribune Foundation; U.S. Bancorp Piper Jaffray Foundation on behalf of U.S. Bancorp Piper Jaffray; and generous individuals.

Library of Congress Cataloging-in-Publication Data

Caldwell, V. M., 1956–
    The ocean within / V. M. Caldwell. — 1st ed.
       p.   cm.
    Summary: When Elizabeth, an eleven-year-old foster child, is adopted by the boisterous, openly affectionate Sheridan family, it is Grandma who decides to use a fresh approach in trying to help her connect with her new family.
    ISBN 1-57131-623-X (hardcover). — ISBN 1-57131-624-8 (paperback)
    [1. Foster home care Fiction.   2. Grandmothers Fiction.   3. Family life Fiction.]   I. Title
PZ7.C1274350c   1999
[Fic]—dc21                               99-13418
                                                 CIP

This book is printed on acid-free paper.

*to my family
and for every kid
who waits*

# The
# Ocean Within

# Chapter One

Elizabeth was going to throw up.

They had been swaying through the countryside for nearly an hour. The uneven motion of the train made her body feel disconnected. There was a metallic taste in her mouth and the beginning of a headache lurked behind her eyes.

The first part of the train ride had been through the city. There had been lots of stops and starts, lots of people getting on and off, and lots of things to look at through the window. Now there were only endless, flat fields of dusty green, lopsided telephone poles, and clumps of scrawny trees. Elizabeth didn't know what kind of trees they were, and she didn't care.

Paul bounced on the seat beside her. He had snapped his gum until his sister, Caroline, had made him spit it out. He had examined scabs on both knees and one elbow and told eight knock-knock jokes. He had bet his cousin Molly a quarter that he could spell anything. She had agreed and he had spelled it: a-n-y-t-h-i-n-g. Molly had groaned and paid up. She'd bet him back that he couldn't keep quiet for sixty seconds. Paul had lost and cheerfully returned the quarter. Now he was swinging his feet and watching his untied shoelaces make patterns in the air. One foot accidentally bumped Elizabeth's leg. She hugged her arms to her stomach and pressed herself farther into the corner.

"How much longer?" Paul asked.

"When we see the water tower, eight minutes." Caroline smiled at her brother. Then she turned her head to include Elizabeth.

"Not too long," added Molly.

She smiled, too, and Elizabeth was struck anew by the family resemblance among the Sheridan cousins. Caroline was fifteen, slender, and a head taller than Elizabeth. Her hair was a rich shade of reddish brown. Her eyes were greenish blue, and her smile began there.

Molly—short for Magdalena, a name she claimed to hate—was thirteen and almost as tall as Caroline. Her hair was black and wavy, and her eyes were a shiny dark brown. But her smile was like Caroline's, and she looked people in the eye the way Caroline did.

The way *all* the Sheridans she'd met did, even Paul.

In appearance, he was a miniature version of his sister. His hair was shorter, and his eyes were perhaps a shade grayer. But Caroline could hold herself still and Paul was always in motion.

"I can't wait to go swimming." Paul sat on both hands and still managed to bounce. "Will Grandma take us right away? As soon as we get there?"

Caroline smiled again. "If she can't, I bet Adam will."

Elizabeth pictured the family portrait in the front hall of Caroline and Paul's house. Adam must be the tallest boy, the one whose hair was black, like Molly's. In the photograph, he was holding a toddler—Elizabeth couldn't remember whether it was a boy or a girl. She hadn't really paid attention when Caroline and Paul had named the people in the picture. For one thing, there were too many of them. For another, it didn't matter.

Karen, Caroline and Paul's mother, had wedged one of Elizabeth's school pictures into a corner of the frame. Before they'd left the house this morning, Elizabeth had jimmied it out. At the train station, she'd thrown it away.

"What *I* can't wait for is cherry cake." Molly licked her lips.

"I'm with you." Caroline turned to Elizabeth. "Grandma's cherry cake is fantastic!"

*You can stop cheerleading now. Your parents aren't here.*

Elizabeth's eyes narrowed. How had Caroline phrased it? "Elizabeth isn't any more of a *sister* than she was the day she moved in!" Elizabeth had overheard Kevin, Caroline and Paul's father, say he was sorry the last seven weeks had been hard, but at least the four of them knew each other. For Elizabeth, a stranger to their family, adjusting must be even harder. They would have to be patient. In a hopeful tone, Karen had added that going to Grandma's was a chance for a fresh start . . .

Elizabeth scowled. She didn't need anyone's pity. *Or* a fresh start.

"Fudge cake's even better," said Paul. "I hope she made that."

Caroline grinned. "Bet she's made both."

"She's an *awesome* cook, Elizabeth. I always gain about ten pounds in July." Molly sighed happily.

Elizabeth knew that if they didn't stop talking about food, she really would get sick. She swallowed hard and looked out the window again. Fields had given way to maple trees. To her enormous relief, Caroline changed the subject.

"Grandma's amazing, Elizabeth. She's smart, and she's funny, and she really listens. She knows how to do just about anything. She can sew and fix cars— at least simple things, like spark plugs." Caroline paused. "And she always knows who needs a hug."

*I hope she knows who doesn't.*

Although she had been at Kevin and Karen's for

almost two months, Elizabeth had not yet met Mrs. Sheridan, Kevin's mother. Kevin and Karen had wanted Elizabeth to have a few weeks to get used to the four of them and to get settled at school. When Paul had gotten pneumonia, Kevin hadn't wanted to risk exposing his mother. Then Rachel, Kevin's sister-in-law, had surgery, and Mrs. Sheridan had gone to look after those grandchildren for two weeks. In the end, it seemed easiest to postpone introductions another week: Elizabeth would meet the Sheridan family matriarch today.

"And Santa Claus *learned* about Christmas from her," said Molly.

"What do you mean? Isn't Santa older than Grandma?"

"It's just an expression, Paul. I meant she really makes Christmas special," Molly assured him. He nodded, apparently satisfied.

"It's hard to describe," Caroline continued thoughtfully. "She's sort of a storybook grandmother, but real. She's strong inside."

"Huh! She's strong *outside*." Paul scowled and rubbed the seat of his shorts. Caroline and Molly started to giggle and, after a moment, Paul grinned.

"I guess we should explain," Caroline said. "Grandma spanks."

"Hard," added Paul. "She makes you bend over her bed, and then *whamo!*"

*He's got to be making this up.*

Elizabeth looked at Caroline and Molly. The expressions on their faces said that he wasn't.

*Do people still do that?*

"It's true." Caroline shrugged. "But don't worry about it. You never do anything wrong." Her eyebrows drew together in a puzzled expression.

"Huh!" Paul said. "*You* get spanked, and you're practically perfect."

"My mother *hates* it that Grandma spanks," Molly said.

Caroline turned to Elizabeth. "Mom hates it, too," she confided. "She thinks it's barbaric."

Paul jumped out of his seat and almost hit Elizabeth in the head as he pointed. "The water tower!"

The Sheridans scrambled to look out the window and Elizabeth retreated into her own thoughts. Eight minutes until they arrived at the station. There would be a twenty-minute drive before they reached the house and all sorts of tedious introductions to endure when they got there. But the moment would come when she could escape, when she could finally do what she had come to do.

This afternoon she would see the ocean.

And she would have four whole weeks to store up memories. Ones she could replay whenever she wished. No matter where she was.

"We're almost there! Paul, tie your shoes. Molly, give me a hand with this thing, would you?" Caroline and Molly struggled to pull an overstuffed bag from under the seat Elizabeth shared with Paul.

"Got it!" cried Molly in triumph. The bag came free and, laughing, the two girls fell backwards. Elizabeth decided that Sheridans could laugh at just about anything.

The train's whistle wailed twice and the screech of its brakes grew louder. To Elizabeth's surprise, the train came to a stop with barely a jerk. She hoped it would be a few minutes before they got into the car. Her stomach needed time to recover.

"I see Adam!" Paul disappeared into a forest of adult legs.

"Sorry, Elizabeth, but could you grab Paul's bag?" Arms full, Caroline struggled forward. "You O.K., Molly? I'm glad I've been lifting weights!"

Elizabeth wished for a moment that *she* had lifted weights. Paul's bag weighed a ton, and it was full of sharp objects. Dragging her own small suitcase behind her, Elizabeth half-jumped, half-fell onto the platform. She righted herself and looked to see which way the others had gone.

Caroline had dropped her bags and was waving enthusiastically to the boy from the picture. He beamed as he came toward her, arms open wide. They hugged each other.

*Why don't these people shake hands, like the rest of the world?*

"*Dah*-ling, you look *mah*-velous!" Adam and

Caroline spoke in perfect unison. Then they burst into laughter.

"Adam, this is Elizabeth. Elizabeth, Cousin Adam—fearless leader of the Sheridan brat pack!"

He turned his radiant smile on her. "Hello, Elizabeth. Welcome to the family!"

# Chapter
# Two

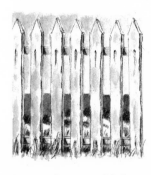

*Four more minutes. Five or six at the most.*

Elizabeth was wedged between Caroline and Molly in the back of the station wagon. She was grateful that Paul was in the front seat, although she didn't see how Adam could drive when Paul kept changing the radio station. Not to mention the fact that all four Sheridans were talking a mile a minute. She tuned out their voices and concentrated on the odors coming through the windows.

She'd seen pictures and movies of the ocean, of course. And her cassette tape of ocean sounds was her most treasured possession. But she had wondered for years how the ocean smelled. Maybe they were close enough now. She closed her eyes and sniffed the warm

breeze. Fresh-cut hay. Diesel fuel. Something sweet . . .
something *purple?*

She blinked. Paul had stuffed his mouth with gum
and the car was full of the smell of artificial grapes.
Elizabeth pressed her lips together and resigned herself to waiting. They passed a gas station, turned right,
and were suddenly in the town.

"Here it is, Elizabeth," Adam cried. "The booming
metropolis of South Wales!"

The others laughed. "Downtown" was three blocks
long and looked like something out of a movie. *The
Music Man*, Elizabeth thought. No billiard parlor, no
livery, but everything else was there: barber shop, grocery store, theater, pharmacy, ice-cream parlor, town
hall, and library. It would not have surprised her to
see a singing quartet in straw hats, but the few people
they saw were dressed in perfectly ordinary clothes,
mostly T-shirts and shorts.

They turned left at the third stop sign, turned
right four blocks later, and pulled into the driveway
of a house that had—Elizabeth could not believe it—
a picket fence. It wasn't white—it was unpainted
wood—but it was a picket fence. They had arrived.

Leaving car doors open, the Sheridans clamored
out. It was a relief to be able to stretch and to be alone
for a moment. Elizabeth took a deep breath. The air
was cooler than it had been at the train station. The
aroma of artificial grapes had been replaced by pine
and . . .

She sat very still. It was a tangy smell. She thought she could taste it. Something about it made her want to take another breath and then another. It was a mixture, she decided. Salt and fish, but other things, too. Things she'd never smelled before. It was mysterious and tantalizing.

"Hey, Elizabeth!" Adam called. "Come and meet everybody!"

Elizabeth sighed. She hated this part.

*Get on with it, Lawson.*

She slid across the seat and climbed out. A swarm of Sheridans chattered and laughed on the lawn. She recognized the porch as the one in the family portrait, but the photograph must have been cropped: the house was wider than she had pictured it.

"This is Abby, and that's Sarah, and the goofball on the railing is Andrew." Adam's dark eyes darted from one side of the porch to the other. "Where's Petey?"

"I'm here." A small boy with a serious expression appeared at the side of the house. He crossed the lawn and gazed up with searchlight eyes of deep blue. "Hello."

*This kid can't be a Sheridan.*

He wasn't loud, he wasn't laughing—he wasn't even smiling. He was just looking at her.

A door banged and Elizabeth turned toward the sound. Paul had someone in a death-grip embrace. The someone squeezed him back. When he released her, she turned to hug Caroline and then Molly.

*Grandma.*

A build somewhere between sturdy and lean. Dark blue, short-sleeved shirt, gray shorts, sneakers. Wavy, dark brown hair with patches of gray, combed casually back. A purposeful walk, a firm step. No glasses, no makeup, no jewelry except for a wristwatch and a narrow wedding band.

There were laugh lines at the corners of her eyes, and she was smiling now, but her dark gaze was intense. Elizabeth resisted the impulse to step backwards. It was one thing to be looked at that way by a young child. It was quite another thing coming from this no-nonsense adult.

"Hello, Elizabeth." Her voice was low. Elizabeth had steeled herself against a hug, but Mrs. Sheridan contented herself with briefly placing a hand on one of Elizabeth's shoulders. "Welcome."

Elizabeth repressed a shudder. Kevin had greeted her with the same quiet directness. She preferred the disinterested reserve or the tactless curiosity to which she was accustomed.

"Can we go swimming, Grandma?" Paul asked. "Pleeeease?"

"Let's get the car unloaded and everybody settled first." Her eyes twinkled. "Ten minutes?"

Mrs. Sheridan grinned as the porch exploded in noise. The older kids hurled themselves toward the car, the two youngest girls squealed and darted into the house, and the little boy—a Sheridan after all—gave a loud *whoop* and ran up the steps.

"Elizabeth, you'll be with Abby and Sarah. We weren't sure you'd like the bunk bed, so we gave you the single bed by the window." Mrs. Sheridan led her into the house and pointed to the left. "Right up those stairs." She gave Elizabeth an encouraging smile. "I'll call Karen so she'll know you've arrived."

Elizabeth's suitcase lay on top of a periwinkle blue bedspread. Forest green spreads covered the bunk beds. Her roommates were putting on bathing suits in front of a wooden bureau. One of them couldn't get her straps straight, and the other one was trying to help.

"That's your dresser." The taller girl pointed to a small white chest of drawers. "Me and Sarah share this one."

*Sarah and I.*

"Hurry up and change, O.K.? We got here this morning, but we haven't been to the beach. Grandma needed to stay here, and she wouldn't let us go without Adam." Abby bent over to pull on her sneakers. "We have to wear shoes till the sand," she explained. "I'll get some towels."

Seconds later, Abby held an olive green towel toward Elizabeth and handed a tan one to Sarah. "Aren't you going to change?"

Elizabeth shook her head.

"You're not going swimming?" Sarah's eyes grew wide.

Elizabeth shook her head again. Abby exchanged a puzzled glance with her sister and shrugged. "C'mon, then. Let's go!"

They clattered down the stairs. Elizabeth laid the towel next to her suitcase and followed them. A horde of Sheridans bombarded her with questions about her lack of a bathing suit.

*They're louder than the* Wilsons!

"That's enough!" Mrs. Sheridan's voice cut through the din. "It's Elizabeth's decision to swim or not to, and she doesn't have to explain it to a bunch of over-curious water rats." Her tone was light and she was smiling, but her eyes said she meant business.

There were murmurs of "O.K., Grandma" and "Sorry, Elizabeth."

"Good. Adam, would you please grab the whistles?"

The Sheridans surged onto the porch and spilled down the steps.

"Forgive their manners, Elizabeth." Mrs. Sheridan smiled again. "'Beach' and 'swimming' are synonymous to them."

Sarah took her grandmother's hand and began to tell her about a trip her class had taken to a dairy farm.

*Thank goodness.*

As they stepped onto the road, Elizabeth's heart pushed its way into her throat.

# Chapter
# Three

The tingle in her nose grew stronger.

There was something challenging in the smell, something that made her feel lighter and larger. A gust of wind carried the oily scent of fish. The next gust smelled of chlorophyll— seaweed or algae?

Walking to one side of Mrs. Sheridan and half a pace behind her, Elizabeth kept her eyes on the ground. She wanted her first view of the ocean to reach all the way to the horizon.

Her skin began to feel damp, and the air tasted of salt. The waves grew louder and her chest began to throb. Their sound was familiar, but it wasn't the same as her tape. These sounds were richer and fuller, the screams of the seagulls more raucous.

They turned left and walked across a patch of stony ground.

"This is it!" Mrs. Sheridan's voice sounded far away.

What if it wasn't as wonderful as she had dreamed? As she had hoped? As she *needed* it to be? Elizabeth filled her lungs and lifted her head.

*Please.*

She opened her eyes.

*It's so* big!

For a long moment she could contemplate nothing but the vastness of the water. It stretched forward and forward and forward. She had never seen such an uninterrupted vista. Far, far away, a straight line separated the gray blue of the water from the pale blue of the sky. To her left, beige sand gave way to small rocks. They became boulders and, beyond them, the ocean disappeared. To her right lay a long, sandy beach. It, too, ended in boulders. Elizabeth could imagine the ocean reaching behind them and going on forever. It was intimidating and exhilarating.

And every part of it was moving. Far from shore, waves flickered into and out of existence. The same spot looked black, then white, then blue, and then gray. Closer to shore, whitecaps were visible among waves that danced. Here, the waves roared onto the beach and hissed their way up the sand.

"Elizabeth?"

She wrenched her eyes from the water and located the voice. It was holding the little boy's hand.

". . . to come and get your feet wet?"

It took Elizabeth a moment to realize what Mrs. Sheridan had said. Her eyes grew wide. Then she shut them tightly and shook her head vehemently.

*Touch it? Touch that seething expanse?*

A violent spasm shook her. She cringed and then forced herself to squint her eyes open. Slowly, jaggedly, she exhaled. The ocean was where she had left it. Several minutes passed before she began to hear the lull of the waves, and several more passed before her muscles began to uncoil.

*I wish I were taller.*

Where had that thought come from? After a moment, she knew. She wanted to see all of this from some higher place. In order to sort things out, she needed perspective.

A clump of boulders offered itself to her left. The largest one would put her only seven or eight feet above the sand, but she decided to try it. Sand clung to the bottoms of her sneakers and she slipped twice, but she made it all the way up and was delighted to find a flat spot on which to sit.

*Tweet! Tweet!* A pause. *Tweet! Tweet!* A distinctly non-ocean sound. Mrs. Sheridan and Adam were standing a few yards from the water's edge. They each wore a blue whistle suspended from a red cord.

Hair plastered and dripping, Sheridans stumbled through the waves and tiptoed onto the sand. They clumped together, postures nearly identical: arms hugging chests, bodies bent at the knees and the waist, weight shifting from one foot to the other. When the last of them joined the huddle, Mrs. Sheridan raised one hand.

"All here!" she called, and they scampered back into the water.

Elizabeth turned to survey the ocean from her new vantage point. Things looked different. Not in the particulars, not in the details of what she saw, but because she felt less overwhelmed, better able to explore. Elbows on her knees, her chin in both hands, she lost herself in the sights and sounds of the ocean.

*Tweet! Tweet! Tweet!* Sheridans shuffled, hopped, and ran from the water to look for sneakers and to fight over towels. Elizabeth reluctantly prepared to abandon her perch. She climbed down carefully, took one last look, and followed them back to the house.

"Wet stuff in the mudroom or on the line," Mrs. Sheridan said. "The job list is on the little refrigerator."

Everyone thundered up the stairs. Not knowing what else to do, Elizabeth shadowed Sarah and Abby to their room and sat on her bed while they changed.

*I've been to the ocean.*

The realization slammed into her.

*I've seen it.*

"You coming, Elizabeth?" Abby stopped in the

doorway. "Do you have a nickname? Betsy or Liz or something?"

Warily, Elizabeth shook her head.

"O.K." Abby smiled and then shrugged. "I just wondered."

Elizabeth followed her down the hall. Through the open door of the next room she saw Paul's bag. She passed the bathroom. She had to go, but she didn't want to say so.

Across from the bathroom stood a linen closet and a rather narrow door, which was closed. Caroline's voice rose and fell behind the last door on the left. The room on the right was immaculate.

*Must be Mrs. Sheridan's.*

They went down a staircase that turned a corner and out through a screen door. At the side of the house, clotheslines zigzagged and drooped under the weight of wet towels.

"You'd think Mr. Mechanic could learn to operate a clothespin." Abby sounded mildly exasperated, but she hummed as she picked up Paul's swimming trunks and pinned them to the line. She added her suit and Sarah's and the towels they had used.

"Andrew did the job list for the whole month," Abby said. "It took him almost an hour. I've got dishes tonight. I think you've got Helping, but we'd better check."

*Helping?*

They went back through the door, up six steps to the left, and into a cheerful kitchen of considerable size. Mrs. Sheridan was standing at the stove. They watched her add something to an enormous aluminum pot and give it a stir.

"Hi, Grandma! What are we having?"

Mrs. Sheridan smiled at Abby. "Hamburgers and veggie sticks and that pasta salad you like so much."

"The one with the olives? Thank you, thank you!"

"And two kinds of dessert!" Andrew set a large cardboard box on the floor and nodded toward the counter. Two cakes waited, one pink and one brown.

"As soon as Andrew gets out of the way, we can check the list," said Abby.

Her brother had opened the box and was piling cans of pop onto the bottom shelf of the refrigerator. One of *two* refrigerators, Elizabeth realized as Mrs. Sheridan stepped away from the stove. The second one was larger. Taped to the front of it was a lopsided drawing of a skull and crossbones. *Beware of Grandma!* was written in shadow letters across the top.

"Andrew, please *stack* those cans. Avalanches are inconvenient and frequently painful."

He gave his grandmother a sheepish grin and started over.

"Abby, why don't you explain Paul's drawing?"

*This woman doesn't miss a thing.*

"Last year, every time Grandma went to cook, somebody had eaten half the stuff she needed. So we got the little fridge — Mr. Ciminelli gave it to us — and now it's for drinks and snacks. Anybody can take things out of the little fridge, but only Grandma can go in the big one."

Andrew closed the door.

"Except if you're Helping." Abby crossed the room to read from a chart that looked like a chessboard. "Which you are."

"That means helping me in the kitchen before dinner. Sometimes it's salad; sometimes it's baking. Tonight, it's carrots." Mrs. Sheridan smiled as she placed a piece of newspaper and a vegetable peeler on the table.

Andrew and Abby disappeared, and Elizabeth became aware that she was uncomfortable being alone with their grandmother. While she worked, Elizabeth watched Mrs. Sheridan out of the corner of her eye. In rapid sequence, Mrs. Sheridan shaped fourteen hamburger patties, drained a bowl of celery, stirred the pot, took nine glasses from a shelf and set them on a tray, stirred the pot again, and placed a colander in the sink.

*To call this woman efficient would be an understatement.*

When she had scraped a dozen carrots, Elizabeth looked up. Mrs. Sheridan gave her a rueful grin. "The whole bag, I'm afraid. The older kids have sumo-wrestler appetites."

When she finished, Mrs. Sheridan provided her

with a cutting board and a sharp blade. Working quickly, Elizabeth sliced the carrots into sticks.

"You're pretty handy with a knife," Mrs. Sheridan said with approval. "Do you mind doing onions?"

Elizabeth shook her head. She diced three onions, a can of black olives, and two jars of green ones. Between onions and olives she witnessed an incredible scene.

Petey walked into the kitchen and over to the sink where his grandmother was draining pasta. He thrust his arms out. Mrs. Sheridan put down the pan, wiped her hands on her shorts, and picked him up. They hugged each other tightly. When he leaned back, she put him down and kissed him on the forehead. They looked into each other's eyes for a moment. Then Petey smiled and walked out of the kitchen — without saying a single word. Matter-of-factly, Mrs. Sheridan picked up the steaming pot and finished pouring its contents into the strainer.

*And I thought Kevin and Karen were odd!*

"Thank you, Elizabeth. You've been a big help. It will take me about twenty minutes to finish up. Why don't you look around out back?"

Through the window Elizabeth saw a small barn partly hidden by pine trees.

*The path of least resistance: do as you're told.*

She went.

# Chapter
# Four

The smell of pine was inviting. Centered among five trees, two log benches faced each other. Elizabeth eased herself down onto one and the afternoon flooded back.

*I've seen the ocean.*

She tried to hear the waves, but couldn't. She stood up and tried again. No luck. Restlessly, she turned toward the barn. It was the same silver gray as the house, but it was made of boards instead of shingles. The door was unlocked. She lifted the latch and stepped inside.

The wooden shutters were closed, but here and there a slender beam of light slipped through a crack or a knothole. A basketball hoop was suspended from the wall on the left. Near it, garden tools hung out of the reach of small children. Against the wall on the right stood a workbench of some sort. Stacks of wood were piled next to and beneath it.

"Eliz-a-beth, din-ner!"

Inside the back door of the house she stopped to listen. They were still carrying things from the kitchen to the dining room. She ran upstairs to the bathroom and back down. From the doorway, she watched the Sheridans serve themselves.

It was obvious that "No, thank you" helpings were the same here as they were at Kevin and Karen's house. You had to take at least one bite of each thing that was offered. If you wanted dessert, you had to eat what you took. Elizabeth put a small portion of each dish on a plate.

"We need to explain how we tell 'bests,'" Mrs. Sheridan said. "Sarah, would you like to do it?"

"We take turns." Her pigtails bounced. "The best thing that happened to you, in the *whole* day, that's what you tell." She grinned at Elizabeth. "Then you say who goes next!"

Elizabeth's eyebrows drew together. Kevin and Karen's house had been the first place she'd stayed where people hadn't watched TV during dinner. Talking was bad enough, but *this* was ridiculous.

"There's a three-sentence limit," Andrew warned. "Otherwise, we'd be here all night."

"Ain't *that* the truth!" Molly moaned, and everyone laughed.

Deliberately, mischievously, Mrs. Sheridan put her hand on the table. Silently, the tribe pleaded. She grinned and lifted her fork. On all sides, silverware clattered against plates.

"Grandma, tell first," said Caroline.

"My best is finally meeting Elizabeth and having all of you here." She paused to smile. "I pass my turn to Molly."

"My best is that you made cherry cake. I drooled my way through exams thinking about it," she confessed. "I pass my turn to Paul."

"Swimming!" he shouted. "I pass my turn to Adam."

"My best . . ." He finished chewing and swallowed. ". . . was being allowed to collect the newest member of the family from the train station." He smiled at Elizabeth. "I pass my turn to Petey."

Petey put down his fork and put both hands in his lap. He tilted his head, contemplated a saltshaker, and nodded once.

"Now," he said simply.

His grandmother smiled at him. "And who gets your turn, Petey?"

"Elizabeth."

*Never let them know what's important to you.*

She flushed and looked down. The dining room had grown uncomfortably quiet.

*Hurry! It's only going to get worse.*

"The noodles." She pointed her fork at the salad which remained on her plate.

"Another vote for your pasta, Abby." Mrs. Sheridan glanced at Elizabeth, turned back to Abby, and added, "Why don't you go next?"

*I saw the ocean. I saw the ocean. I saw the ocean. I saw the ocean.*

Elizabeth lost herself in the realization that it had actually happened, that the waiting and wondering were over. She had made it, and it had been even more than she'd hoped for. She didn't hear the others finish telling their bests or see Caroline remove her plate. It wasn't until Andrew nudged her and pointed toward the head of the table that she came out of her reverie.

"Cherry or chocolate or both?" Mrs. Sheridan held a cake server in one hand.

Elizabeth shook her head.

"No, thank you?"

"No, thank you," she echoed.

"You're nuts, Elizabeth," said Paul. "You don't know what you're missing."

"Paul." The warning was unmistakable.

"Sorry," he said quickly.

Amid compliments to the chef, both cakes disappeared. They looked good, but Elizabeth felt no desire to change her mind.

*I've seen the ocean.*

She had realized a dream, one she had harbored and nursed for nearly five years. She was full.

The family settled itself into the large space that they called the front room. Elizabeth chose a chair next to a window and began to catalogue the Sheridans she'd met today.

On the floor, next to Caroline, was Abby: nine or ten, hazel eyes, dark brown hair with red highlights, forthright. Next to her was Paul. Next to him sat Sarah: six or seven, medium-brown hair streaked with blond, eyes somewhat darker than Abby's, bouncy. The older kids were explaining a board game to her.

On a sofa built for six people, Molly was reading to Petey: three or four, wavy hair the color of sand, those disconcerting blue eyes, thoughtful. *Too* thoughtful for someone his size.

Adam was standing by the stone fireplace. Seventeen? Eighteen? Black hair, watchful dark brown eyes, a determined chin. Taller than his grandmother, more an adult than one of the kids. Laughing at something he'd said was Andrew. Andrew was only three inches shorter than Adam, but the softness of his cheeks suggested he was much younger. Thirteen? He must be—Kevin and Karen had scheduled Elizabeth's second visit around his bar mitzvah. Sandy hair like Petey's, hazel eyes like Abby's. What else? Elizabeth wasn't sure.

Her eyes lingered on Andrew, reluctant to complete the inventory. To her right, Mrs. Sheridan smiled quietly as she mended a pair of red-and-black shorts. She wore glasses to sew and looked over them frequently. Her eyes flickered around the room and back to her task. Outside, in the sunlight, her eyes had looked brown. In the kitchen, they had looked blue. Elizabeth decided now they were slate colored, a dark bluish gray.

Having launched the younger kids on the board game, the older ones decided on Scrabble. Both games were played with Sheridan vigor and volume. Elizabeth watched Molly add "l-a-m" to "bed." Then she realized with a start that Petey was standing next to her.

"How old are you?"

Elizabeth was aware that Mrs. Sheridan was watching them. She wished something would make her stop.

"Eleven."

"That's what they said. But you seem older." He continued to look at her.

"How old are *you*?" she finally asked.

"Four." He smiled, and his whole face lit up.

*He's a Sheridan.*

"My birthday was last week. Right, Grandma?"

She grinned at him. "Pretty neat to be four, isn't it?"

"I'm still the youngest," he said, slowly. "But I'm not the *newest* anymore." He smiled again. "*You* are!"

With that happy thought, he went up the stairs. He returned with a toy car in each hand and drove them back and forth between Elizabeth's feet and those of his grandmother until she announced it was bedtime.

Elizabeth waited her turn outside the bathroom. Through the partly opened door of Andrew and Paul's room she heard Andrew say, "Your new sister doesn't talk much, does she?"

"Nope. She's shy." Paul answered cheerfully. "But she's all right," he added in a challenging tone.

"I didn't say she *wasn't*, pinhead!"

A series of *whaps* and bursts of laughter told her a pillow fight had begun. Molly emerged from the bathroom and Elizabeth went in, closing the door against the clamor of family life.

*I've seen the ocean.*

She examined herself in the mirror. Hair still dishwater blond, still straight, still shoulder length. Eyes still the dull, dark tan of November leaves. Nose and mouth still present. Pointed chin in its usual place at the bottom of her thin face.

*I feel different. Why don't I look different?*

"Hurry up, Elizabeth!" Sarah hollered. "I have to *go!*"

Scowling, Elizabeth brushed her teeth and withdrew down the hall. At least at the Hartricks' there had been more than one bathroom.

The bunk bed swayed as Abby climbed the ladder, and Elizabeth was grateful that she'd been given the single bed. She peered into the night through the screen. Lined by pine trees, the driveway lay to her right. In front of her and to the left, more pines blocked any possible view of the ocean. A triangle of porch was visible where railings met the the corner post.

*This window has potential.*

Sarah banged through the bedroom door and jumped onto the lower bunk.

"If this thing falls down, *you're* the one who's gonna get squished," Abby warned.

"Ready, girls?" Mrs. Sheridan came into the room. "Teeth brushed?"

"Yes!" Abby and Sarah crawled under their covers.

"Summer is my favorite time," Sarah said happily.

Her grandmother kissed her. "Mine, too."

"Can we go swimming right after breakfast tomorrow?"

"As soon as jobs are finished." Mrs. Sheridan tucked the blanket around Abby's shoulders and gave her a kiss.

"Hop in, Elizabeth." Mrs. Sheridan watched her from the doorway.

*Karen must have warned her. Thank goodness.*

"Sweet dreams." The light went off and the door clicked closed.

The silence lasted less than a second.

"Why didn't Grandma kiss you?" Sarah demanded.

"Sarah!" her sister scolded. "That's *personal.*"

"It is?" Sarah squeaked. "How come?"

"I'll explain in the morning. Go to sleep, now, O.K.?"

"O.K. Good night."

"Good night."

Elizabeth waited. When she heard regular breathing from both bunks, she reached down to her suitcase. Her fingers felt among the clothes until they found her pouch. She picked it up, tightened its drawstring, and slid it into the far corner of her pillowcase. Having completed her arrival-night task—she'd lost count of the times she had done so—she pulled up the blanket.

*It really happened. I've seen the ocean.*

She sighed, a mixture of satisfaction and awe.

*I'm not the same person I was this morning.*

# Chapter
# Five

The Sheridan kids served themselves cereal and bacon and toast much more quietly than they had served dinner. Five minutes into the meal, they began to talk. Five minutes later, they began to laugh. Five minutes after that, they were communicating at the previous night's volume and Elizabeth was reminded of the train station.

Plates were soon empty of everything but silverware, but no one asked to be excused. Instead, they smiled at each other. Finally, Mrs. Sheridan looked at the ceiling.

"I suppose it's too much to hope for," she said in a sad, wistful voice, "but did *anyone* get promoted this year?" The throng burst again into happy chatter.

*They've done this before.*

Adam and Caroline and Andrew each passed her

a handful of paper. In Caroline's pile, Elizabeth recognized her report card. She cringed.

*I don't want her to see that!*

She'd had A's in everything except English. That grade had been a B. She would have had an A except that she had refused to write an autobiography. She didn't even care what the report card said. It was just personal.

*Do these people share everything?*

Mrs. Sheridan shuffled the papers and put on her glasses. "Sarah first." She read for a moment and smiled. "Beautiful, Sarah. I especially like the comment about listening." She took a bank envelope from her pocket. "Second grade in September?"

Sarah nodded happily and Mrs. Sheridan handed her two new dollar bills.

"Thank you, Grandma!"

To Elizabeth's horror, Mrs. Sheridan then gave Sarah's report card to Andrew. He read it, passed it to Molly, and whispered something to Sarah. She smiled again.

"You really worked hard this year, didn't you, Paul?" He blushed and grinned. "This is terrific." Mrs. Sheridan seemed as pleased with his C's and one B as Kevin and Karen had been. She counted out four singles, passed them to Paul, and handed his report card to Andrew.

*Stop it!*

"How did you do this year, Abby?"

Elizabeth looked around the table. Hers would be next.

"May I be excused?" Her voice burst forth, higher and louder than she had intended.

Mrs. Sheridan stopped reading. After a moment, she nodded. "You may."

As quickly as she could, Elizabeth slipped between the chairs. She walked upstairs to the bedroom and sat on the floor next to the window.

*How could they do that, without even asking?*

It was bad enough that Kevin and Karen had looked at it. The Wilsons, the Hartricks, *none* of the others had asked to see her report cards. A salty gust of wind came through the screen and she took a deep breath. It wasn't right, and it wasn't fair, but it wasn't the end of the world. What mattered was the ocean. If she stayed focused on it, she'd manage to cope.

Abby and Sarah burst through the door. They dropped their report card money into the top drawer of their dresser and darted to the bunk bed.

"Hurry, Elizabeth," Abby said. "We can swim as soon as jobs are done. You've got dishes. I checked."

There was frenzied activity all along the hall and it was a relief to reach the comparative calm of the kitchen. Andrew was sweeping and his grandmother was wiping the stove with a sponge.

"We've got a system for dishes that works pretty well. Andrew, would you please explain it?" Mrs. Sheridan went up the back stairs.

"We're a high-volume operation. It saves water if we do it like this." Andrew filled a dishpan with hot water and soap and explained the order in which to rinse silverware, glasses, and plates. He gave her a curious half-smile and followed his grandmother.

*Not exactly brain surgery.*

Elizabeth was putting knives and spoons into the dishwasher when Mrs. Sheridan returned. She was wearing an apologetic smile.

"It never occurred to me that our report card ritual would make you uncomfortable. I'm sorry that it did." She laid a five dollar bill and two singles on the counter. "Here's your share of the bank."

Elizabeth started to shake her head. Then she remembered the dinner table. "No, thank you." She took another handful of silverware from the dishpan.

Mrs. Sheridan looked at Elizabeth with an expression she couldn't read and tucked the money into her pocket. "I'll hold on to it for you. Are you planning to swim this morning?"

Elizabeth shook her head.

"Then meet us on the porch when you're finished."

*Something just happened, but I don't know what.*

The dishpan was empty. Elizabeth poured the gray water down the drain, rinsed the pan, and closed the dishwasher door. As she dried her hands, her eye caught Paul's skull drawing.

*Beware of Grandma.*

Elizabeth walked behind the others, struggling to control the turmoil within her. Yesterday hadn't been a dream. She had seen the ocean, and she was going to see it again.

*My heart's beating even faster today . . .*

The morning breeze was cool. The smell of the water was fainter, thinner than it had been in the middle of the afternoon.

*The waves are bigger. Why?*

She shivered as she climbed to yesterday's lookout. The sky was pale blue and the water looked gray. Whitecaps sparkled everywhere. The waves hit the beach with demanding crashes, and the foam skidded across the sand more rapidly than she remembered.

This was surely the ocean she had seen yesterday. It had to be. How could it look so different? It was intriguing and somehow disturbing.

"Hey, Elizabeth!" Adam smiled up at her. Petey was sitting on Adam's shoulders, and the others were straggling toward them. "Time for lunch."

She blushed and climbed down.

"You watching for whales or something?" Molly asked.

Still blushing, Elizabeth shook her head.

"Pirates?" Sarah suggested as they stepped onto the road.

She shook her head again.

"That's enough questions," Mrs. Sheridan said lightly.

The tribe began to talk about friends they had met at the beach and Elizabeth let her mind wander. She'd never had friends, but she'd had her dream of seeing the ocean. That had been better: fascinating, but safe. Always there, never making demands. Her dream had never let her down, and no one had been able to take it away.

But as much as she had read, as many pictures as she had seen, she had been unprepared for the ocean itself. It was so much bigger and louder than she had expected, and the wind and the water never stopped moving. It was a hundred times more beautiful than she had imagined . . . and a hundred times more dangerous. She glanced over her shoulder and shivered.

*What will it look like next time?*

"Caroline, please call the others. And would you bring down the Just-in-Case things? I'd like to have them all in one place."

Elizabeth recognized the envelope that Caroline handed to her grandmother: it contained letters of permission for emergency medical treatment. Because she was a ward of the state, she had needed a second letter. She wasn't sure why that bothered her, but it did.

When everyone had been served, Mrs. Sheridan congratulated them all on a terrific start to the summer and suggested a game of I Spy. The rest of lunch was filled with pointing and questions and wild guesses and laughter. Elizabeth couldn't wait to leave the table.

The afternoon program was a pilgrimage to the library. Another house rule: everyone had to read for at least thirty minutes each day. Elizabeth loved to read and hated being told that she *had* to.

*This place has more rules than the last three combined!*

She fumed silently during the walk into town.

The librarian was a fussy little woman with red hair that escaped in all directions from a lopsided bun. She rummaged in a drawer for a library card application and slid a dog-eared piece of cardboard across the counter. Elizabeth penned her name in careful, vertical letters: *Elizabeth Lawson*. Because Elizabeth was not a permanent resident of South Wales, Mrs. Sheridan was also required to sign. Quickly, she wrote *Martha W. Sheridan* in a small, neat script that slanted toward the right. There was more fussing and waiting while the librarian typed the card. Looking doubtful, she finally allowed Elizabeth to sign it.

Via an indirect route, Elizabeth made her way to section "QH." She found six unfamiliar titles, two of which were especially tempting: *Oceans and Shores* and *Saltwater Haven*. She fingered their spines for a moment, wandered toward Young Adult Fiction, and selected three books she'd already read.

The entire trip home was filled with questions. What had Elizabeth chosen? Had she ever read this one? Did she like that author? Didn't she hate the way that book had ended?

*Don't these people ever stop talking?*

Mrs. Sheridan declared a forty-five-minute inter-mission in which to explore the books they had borrowed, and the house was soon pleasantly quiet. Elizabeth lay on her bed, *A Swiftly Tilting Planet* open in front of her. She wished there had been time to look at the ocean books, especially the one called *Saltwater Haven*. She didn't know what it was about, but she liked the title. It sounded like her rock: a refuge, a place to be safe for a while.

*Especially from Sheridan questions.*

# Chapter
# Six

 Elizabeth was standing in
the dining room trying to
decide where to spend the
time before dinner. She
jumped once when the telephone rang and again when
Mrs. Sheridan called her into the kitchen.

"It's for you." She smiled. "It's Kevin."

Elizabeth took a step backwards, shook her head,
and darted toward the front of the house. Voices
floated through the porch window and she paused.
Were they leaving? Annoyance washed over her as
she realized that she had failed to stay alert to sounds
from the other direction.

"Elizabeth, may I see you for a moment?" Mrs.
Sheridan walked into the dining room.

*Do as you're told. Say as little as possible.*

Elizabeth stopped in the archway and fixed her
eyes on the edge of the table.

"Why did you refuse to speak to Kevin just now?"

Elizabeth shrugged very slightly.

"He was hoping your first day had gone well. That you like it here. That your cousins hadn't overwhelmed you."

Elizabeth stood very still.

"He needed to hear about those things from you, not from me."

*Why is she making a big deal out of this?*

"Kevin and Karen not only care about you, they are responsible for you. From now on, when they call, you will speak to them. Understood?"

Elizabeth clenched her teeth and nodded.

"Look at me, please." Mrs. Sheridan's charcoal gaze was steadfast and expectant.

*Iron Woman.*

Elizabeth nodded a second time.

"Good." Mrs. Sheridan turned toward the kitchen. "The others are just starting a game of croquet. Why don't you join them?"

Scowling, Elizabeth walked onto the porch. Caroline, Molly, and Andrew were setting up wickets and arguing about which way they should face. Sarah was showing Petey how to hit balls with a mallet. He accidentally connected, a green-and-white ball rolled several feet, and they both laughed in surprise. Caroline smiled at them, noticed Elizabeth, and asked her if she wanted to play.

*I need to think, not play some stupid game.*

She shook her head and thumped down the steps. The barn! She reached the clotheslines before she noticed that Abby and Paul were already there.

Her eyes swept back and forth. On the other side of the flapping, damp towels, where the mudroom met the house, was a small alcove. She ducked around the clotheslines and squatted down to check the view.

*Not bad!*

The towels formed a rough semicircle around her. She could see under and between them, and there was just enough room to spot anyone who came out the back door. Unless someone were actively searching for her, she wouldn't be noticed. She placed her back against the wall, hugged her knees to her chest, and put on her cloak of invisibility.

Elizabeth tried to think about the ocean, but she couldn't stay focused. The back of her neck began to feel prickly and she glared at the grass. It was Mrs. Sheridan's fault. It was none of *her* business whether or not she talked to Kevin. And now she would *have* to. How had she been trapped? Elizabeth replayed their conversation and shook her head. She hadn't spoken a single word!

*Iron Woman.*

Mrs. Sheridan made her uncomfortable even when she wasn't being taken to task. It was satisfying to have a designation for her. Elizabeth felt safer, more in control. It was like putting a label on a box.

The back door banged and Adam carried a bag

of charcoal past the corner of the house. Elizabeth leaned down and followed his sneakers to the picnic table. He set the bag down and took the top off the barbecue. She sat up again. She could tell what he was doing by listening. He dumped in the charcoal, replaced the grill, squirted lighter fluid, and lit a match. The result must have satisfied him: he disappeared and the back door slammed.

Elizabeth decided to move before he returned. She knelt on one knee, heard voices, and sat down again. Paul and Abby had come down from the barn.

All was quiet for a moment. She crouched down and watched Paul and Abby walk to the grill. Paul picked up the lighter fluid, raised his eyebrows, and looked at Abby. She shook her head, but she grinned. Paul squeezed the can with both hands. A thin stream of clear liquid arched onto the grill and exploded in flame.

"Oooh! Let me try!"

Paul handed her the can. Abby squeezed hard, and an even bigger flame appeared. Elizabeth heard it sizzle. She wanted to look away but could not. Her heart pounded as she watched them each take another turn.

"Get away from there!"

Elizabeth shrank against the house.

"*Now!*"

Abby and Paul backed away from the grill as Adam charged toward them. He slammed a tray of meat onto the picnic table, snatched the can from Abby's hands, and flipped down the nozzle. "Are the two of you *nuts?*"

The door banged again and Mrs. Sheridan crossed the grass to where Adam glowered at Abby and Paul. Sarah followed her out of the house but stopped next to the table.

"What happened?"

Adam muttered something and waved the can at Abby and Paul. Then he stomped to the grill and began to slam hot dogs and sausages onto hot metal. Smoke billowed, turning his black hair a dull gray. Sarah squinted and blinked and watched him in silence.

Mrs. Sheridan spoke to Abby and Paul for several minutes. Then she pointed toward the house. She paused to say something to Adam, and then the door banged again.

"Are Abby and Paul gonna get spanked?" Sarah looked up at Adam.

"I certainly hope so!" he growled.

Sarah's chin quivered and Adam put down the tongs.

"C'mere, Sair-Bear." He picked her up, gently set her in the middle of the picnic table, and leaned on his elbows. "Do you know what they were doing?"

She shook her head and he explained.

"It was very, very dangerous, Sair. They could have gotten really, really hurt. *Burned.*"

Sarah's eyes grew wide.

"Getting spanked will help them remember never to do it again."

She gazed at him steadily and then nodded.

"I yelled because I was scared." He gave Sarah a kiss. "It's almost time to eat. See if you can find Petey."

Sarah scurried off the table. Adam reached for the tongs and disappeared in another cloud of smoke. The back door banged and Mrs. Sheridan appeared with a platter.

"I'm sorry. I should have been watching."

She shook her head. "You can't be everywhere, Adam. They broke a rule, and they're both old enough to know better." She rubbed a spot between his shoulders. "Almost ready?"

He nodded. She set the platter on the table and Adam began to fork meat from the grill. When the door banged again, Elizabeth crept from her hiding place and ran around to the porch.

"Dinner!" Caroline called.

Elizabeth heard Adam's low voice in the kitchen. A moment later, he came into the dining room with Abby and Paul. Adam looked like himself, but Abby's eyes were bright and Paul's cheeks were flushed.

Iron Woman raised her fork and dinner began. Andrew's best had been beating Adam in a race. Petey's best was finding a crab, and Molly's was that her friends "the twins" had arrived in South Wales. Iron Woman said hers was that Kevin had called,

Adam's best was that Abby and Paul hadn't gotten hurt, and Caroline's was that she had found a ring she'd lost two years ago. Elizabeth chose the sausage. Sarah's best was having helped Grandma make the dessert, Paul chose swimming, and Abby chose a library book. Bests were finished and everyone seemed to be talking at once.

Elizabeth stayed alert enough to monitor the conversations around her while she considered how to contend with Iron Woman. It definitely helped to have labeled her. She was just another adult, and Elizabeth would figure her out. It was only as an unknown quantity that Iron Woman was dangerous.

The direct approach was impossible: Elizabeth could never engage her in conversation. Indirect observation was slower but safer. Elizabeth would study the ways the Sheridan kids dealt with their grandmother. It might take a day or two, but it was better than spending the month looking over her shoulder.

Petey? Tough place to start. Half their communication seemed to take place without words. He adored Iron Woman; she adored him. Nothing useful there.

Sarah? She whined to Andrew and Abby, but not to Iron Woman. Whenever she had the opportunity, she shared every aspect of her life with her grandmother. She also sought her approval.

*Over my dead body.*

Paul? She looked at him. He was telling a tall tale, and he grinned when his grandmother laughed. He didn't look as though he resented her. Then again, she didn't think Paul was *capable* of holding a grudge.

Abby? She was talking to the others, but she looked distracted. Every once in a while, she glanced at her grandmother with a puzzled expression. Abby was worth watching.

Andrew? He bantered with his grandmother as though she were one of the boys, but he also treated her with child-adult deference. He never seemed to be in disfavor. She'd watch Andrew.

Molly? She could be sarcastic, but never directly to Iron Woman, and rarely in her presence. Other than that, she seemed unselfconscious. Elizabeth might learn something from her.

Caroline? Not likely. She spoke of her grandmother with something approaching reverence.

Adam? No help there, either. He was practically her colleague. Wait. Maybe he was worth watching for that reason. She'd consider it.

Dessert was served and dinner was over. The Sheridans who weren't washing dishes gathered in the front room or on the porch. Elizabeth cleared the table and climbed the back stairs. She didn't want to risk being asked to say anything or play anything.

In the hall, she was startled to see the narrow door next to the linen cupboard open. Petey came through it wearing blue-and-white dinosaur pajamas.

*Petey sleeps in a closet?*

He saw her, or sensed her. "Hello."

"Hi."

Cautiously, she walked forward and peered through the door. Eight or ten steps led up to a very small attic room. Its ceiling of unfinished wood sloped sharply. There appeared to be two sources of light, but she could see nothing else.

"That's the Crow's Nest," Petey said. "Where me and Adam sleep. Want to see it?"

Slowly, she shook her head no.

"Are you tired?"

Elizabeth thought about it for a moment. She *was* tired. Very tired.

*Who is this small creature?*

His intense blue gaze had not wavered. She nodded twice, and he nodded back. A moment later, a little wrinkle appeared between his eyebrows.

"Do you have to go?"

Elizabeth shook her head. Petey gave her a lightning smile and hurried into the bathroom. When she heard his bare feet go down to the front room, she put on her pajamas and checked her pillowcase. Her pouch was still there.

She was reading when Abby and Sarah came into the bedroom.

"Abby?" Sarah asked. "Are you O.K.?"

Her sister nodded.

"You're so quiet." Sarah hesitated. "Are you mad at Grandma?"

"No." Abby shook her head impatiently. "I'm just thinking about something she said."

*Definitely worth watching.*

A few minutes later, Iron Woman came to say good night. She leaned down to kiss Sarah first. When Iron Woman stood up, Abby asked her something in a quiet voice. Her response was inaudible.

"What's the difference?"

Again, Iron Woman's reply was too low to hear. She finished speaking and tipped her head to one side.

Abby sat still for a moment. Then her forehead relaxed and she nodded. Her grandmother lifted the blanket and she slid underneath it. Iron Woman smoothed her dark hair, kissed her, and said good night.

What had Elizabeth learned that was useful? Not much, she decided. Iron Woman apparently didn't mind answering questions.

*But I wouldn't ask her anything anyway.*

# Chapter
## Seven

Elizabeth woke up thinking about Iron Woman.

She had one talent at her disposal and she intended to use it. She was an eavesdropper, and she was a professional. An expert amateur, perhaps: she didn't do it for money, and she didn't do it for other people. She eavesdropped because she needed to know things. She did it because it gave her a measure of control. She did it because she loathed surprises of any kind.

Through practice and planning, she'd gotten good at it. She stood downwind, she left doors ajar, and she could stretch a three-minute task to seven or eight. She positioned herself for immediate flight, and she had stories ready in case of discovery. Her cloak of invisibility would serve her well at the

Sheridans'. Ironically, it worked best in a crowded room.

Eavesdropping had been easy at school. Teachers didn't notice if you listened—they barely noticed if you were present. The Wilsons and the Hartricks had been oblivious. They hadn't been very smart, and they hadn't cared who heard what they said.

It was going to be different here. Elizabeth didn't like the Sheridans, but she had to acknowledge that they were intelligent. She had the feeling they wouldn't like being spied on, either. Yesterday, she had simply been looking for a place to be by herself, but she was glad she hadn't been discovered.

Today, she had a mission. Iron Woman had to be deciphered as soon as possible: there were only thirty-one ocean days left.

Family life assaulted her at breakfast. It started with the loud sharing of overnight thoughts and proceeded downhill to family jokes. Molly told a story that ended with the line, "And that's why . . ." The entire family joined her: ". . . we take our umbrellas!" The chorus then burst into sidesplitting laughter.

*What could possibly be funny about umbrellas?*

Elizabeth lost track of the conversation as she tried to imagine the answer. When Elizabeth brought her thoughts back to the table, Iron Woman was remonstrating with Caroline.

"Helen Davenport may not be pleasant . . ." Her grandmother raised one eyebrow.

"I know," Caroline said in a penitent voice. "Not everyone is as lucky as we are."

Elizabeth could tell from her tone that this was another family saying. While she was at Kevin and Karen's house she had dubbed them "Sheridanisms." She found them extremely annoying.

The tribe had started back to the house before Elizabeth climbed down from her rock. Petey had something in his hands and his grandmother's complete attention. Elizabeth strained to hear what they were saying but could not. She had been concentrating hard and was startled when Andrew called to them from the road.

"Grandma, Uncle Steve's on the phone. It's not an emergency, but he said he would wait."

"Elizabeth, please walk back with Petey." Iron Woman hurried across the sand.

After Petey had dumped the sand out of his sneakers and had wedged his feet into them, he looked up at Elizabeth. She crouched down to tie his laces, and then they walked for two blocks in silence. When she heard Petey's voice, Elizabeth's thoughts returned from the ocean.

"How come you never go swimming?"

She glared at the pavement.

*How come you ask so many questions?*

"Don't you *like* the water?" He peered up at her with concern.

She shook her head and was relieved when he walked the rest of the way without speaking.

Elizabeth stood at the bottom of the stairs and listened through the screen door. Molly was describing something that had happened in history class. She told the tale well; she had a definite flair for accents and timing. Caroline giggled frequently, and when Molly reached the punch line, Iron Woman laughed out loud.

*Not a thing to be learned from that.*

Elizabeth was folding laundry in the mudroom. She heard muffled words coming from the kitchen, and she listened closely. It seemed that Andrew had been elected president of the chess club at school.

"That's quite an honor, Andrew." Elizabeth heard water running, a pause, and then: "You don't seem very happy about it."

"There's this guy. Hal. He's first board. Then Netta, then me." He paused. "How big do you want these potatoes?"

"About like this. Is Hal the problem?"

"Yeah." Elizabeth could hear chopping. "When he beat Netta, he cheated."

"You saw him?" Iron Woman asked sympathetically.

"Netta's a better player than Hal. When they posted the list, I asked her how he had won. She'd called time to go to the bathroom, and while she was gone, he moved one of his bishops. She didn't realize it until she was going over the game in her head."

Iron Woman's footsteps neared the stairs. Elizabeth ducked into the mudroom, quickly folded three shirts, and crept back into the hall.

". . . Netta?"

"She asked me not to. And she's right. She can't prove it."

"But you're sure that he did."

"Positive."

Iron Woman's words echoed inside the refrigerator. ". . . big picture. What else would you like to accomplish as president?"

Andrew's voice became animated. "To get more people to try chess. To show them it's fun, and there's strategy, and you don't have to be a genius to play. I thought maybe we could start a junior team for fifth graders and add chess to intramural activities."

"You've given this a lot of thought, haven't you? Is there any way you can solve the problem with Hal and accomplish some of those other things at the same time?"

The telephone rang. Elizabeth folded six pairs of shorts while she waited for the conversation to resume.

". . . an open tournament. With monitors!"

"Sounds good. Any problem getting it scheduled?"

"There shouldn't be. Not if I write to Mr. Dehearna now."

"Help yourself to paper, if you'd like. I'll bet the school's address is on your report card."

"Thanks, Grandma."

*I know more about Andrew, but I haven't learned a thing about Iron Woman.*

Elizabeth frowned as she put on her pajamas. Operation Iron Woman was off to a slow start. Iron Woman had looked carefully at what Petey had found, she had laughed at Molly's story, and she had listened to Andrew's problem. None of that was very helpful: her grandchildren had *wanted* her to look and to laugh and to listen. Elizabeth's problem was defending herself against *unwanted* notice.

*I'll do better tomorrow. I have to.*

Dew soaked through Elizabeth's sneakers. The clatter of porcelain and the smell of cinnamon drifted through the window.

"What *you* know about *women*," Molly snorted, "would fit on the back of a stamp."

"It's a little early to be fighting, isn't it?"

*Iron Woman.*

"She's got PMS or something," Adam grumbled.

"And *your* excuse is . . . ?"

There was a pause; then the three of them laughed. *Worthless.*

Elizabeth carried the last of the breakfast dishes from the dining room to the kitchen. Abby was loading the dishwasher and Iron Woman was making pudding.

"But how do you *know?*"

"You can't know. Not for sure." Iron Woman gave Abby a gentle smile. "People don't come with instruction manuals."

Elizabeth wandered onto the porch wishing she had heard more.

"You know how much I rely on you, Adam . . ."

Elizabeth flattened herself against the bedroom wall and peered down through the screen. Adam was leaning over the handlebars of a bicycle.

". . . but this is your vacation, too. You shouldn't feel as though you're on family duty twenty-four hours a day."

"I don't."

His grandmother folded her arms. "And I'm an armadillo."

Adam laughed.

"Go. Have fun." She smiled. "We'll be here when you get back."

"Better be." He grinned, gave her a kiss, and rode down the driveway.

*Nothing useful in that.*

"Hey, Elizabeth!" Paul had a box in his hands. Chinese checkers, his favorite game. "Want to play?"

She shook her head.

"At home, you always had school stuff to do," he said plaintively. "Why won't you play now?"

She shrugged and turned away.

"You just don't like me." He shoved the box onto a shelf. "Fine! I won't ask you again." His gray green eyes glistened. "Just 'cuz I'm not good at school doesn't mean that I'm stupid."

The screen door slammed.

*It's just a game!*

Iron Woman stepped past her and Elizabeth jumped.

*Where did she come from?!*

Elizabeth fled to her room. Her heart continued to pound as she looked out the window. Iron Woman's arms were wrapped around Paul. There were tears on his cheeks.

*I didn't say he was stupid. I didn't say I didn't like him. I didn't say anything at all!*

Paul shook his head twice. Iron Woman took his chin in her hand, kissed his forehead, and spoke. He nodded, she put her arm around his shoulders, and they walked toward the house.

The throng waited on the porch. When Iron Woman came through the door, it teemed onto the lawn.

"Elizabeth? Walk with me, please?"

Her stomach knotted.

*Do as you're told.*

They waited at the bottom of the steps until the others had made it to the end of the driveway.

"Paul's feeling pretty low."

*I didn't do anything.*

"He thinks you don't like him."

*I never said that.*

"Is he right?"

Elizabeth shook her head.

"Have you ever played a game with Paul?"

She shook her head again.

"Why not?"

Elizabeth shrugged. She didn't play games. What was the point?

"He needs to find some way to connect with you."

*Connect? What is she talking about?*

"If you don't want to play games, will you find something else you can do together?"

*Tell them what they want to hear and they'll leave you alone.*

She nodded.

"Good. It would probably help if you gave him a bit of breathing room first. Tomorrow?"

She nodded again. When they arrived at the sand, Iron Woman turned a brief smile in her direction and went to join her grandchildren.

Elizabeth climbed to her lookout. Once again, Iron Woman had trapped her. Once again, she'd agreed to do something she did not want to do. And, once again, she hadn't spoken a word while it happened.

A feeling of desperation crept into her. It refused to go away, and she brooded for the rest of the afternoon.

Elizabeth was savoring a moment of privacy.

"She never says *anything*, Abby!" Molly's voice carried from the clotheslines to the bathroom window. "How can you stand having her as a roommate?"

"I don't have much choice, do I?"

There was a pause.

"I suppose not," Molly said bleakly. "Even if Grandma said you could move in with us, we couldn't leave poor Sair all alone."

*Business as usual, Lawson.*

After dinner they all walked to the Tiny Theater. It was small, indeed: perhaps fifty seats altogether. It offered a different film every other day and never showed anything that wasn't at least thirty years old. Tonight's movie was a comedy called *Horse Feathers*. Elizabeth appreciated one or two of the puns but disliked everything else. The Sheridans adored it. Iron Woman laughed through the entire thing.

*It's chaos! Why do they think that's funny?*

Elizabeth considered the question as they walked home. There were decidedly Marx Brothers aspects to life at the Sheridans'. Perhaps they'd enjoyed it because it was familiar.

Elizabeth sat on her bed and thought about what she had learned in the course of the day. Or, more accurately, what she *hadn't* learned.

"All set?"

She watched Iron Woman kiss Sarah and Abby.

"Good night, girls."

Iron Woman gave Elizabeth an enigmatic smile and turned off the light.

*"People don't come with instruction manuals."*

It took Elizabeth a very long time to fall asleep.

# Chapter
# Eight

 There was something funny about the way everyone looked at her during breakfast, and Elizabeth suspected that only their grandmother's presence prevented them from asking questions. She was right. When Iron Woman went into the kitchen, Sarah whispered loudly to Caroline, "Maybe she doesn't know."

*Know what?*

She glanced around the table. What was odd about the way they all looked? Something tickled the back of her brain. Iron Woman came back into the room and then she knew. They were all wearing red, white, and blue. It was the Fourth of July.

*Twenty-nine ocean days left!*

Elizabeth lost herself for a moment in the

uncomfortable thought, and then forced herself to focus on the voice at the head of the table.

". . . swim this afternoon, we're all going to rest. You don't have to sleep, but everyone needs to lie down for a while. Fireworks won't begin until close to nine-thirty."

*Fireworks? In person? Not on TV?*

Elizabeth finished sweeping the kitchen and wandered out the back door. She was startled to see Paul sitting at the picnic table with a book. He was savagely carving a line on one page with the point of a pencil. When the door banged, his head snapped up.

"What do *you* want?" he snarled.

Elizabeth shook her head. Abruptly, he turned away and began to carve a new line. A moment later he slammed the book shut and shoved it across the table. It fell onto the grass, and Paul put his head down on his arms. Without thinking, Elizabeth walked around the table and picked up *Basic Skills in Mathematics, Level 3*.

"I *hate* that stupid book, I *hate* stupid math, and I hate *Grandma*."

Elizabeth's eyes widened.

"I have to do three whole *pages* before I can swim. And they have to be right!"

Kevin and Karen had made a deal with Paul. He had to do two pages every day, but if he finished the book, he would earn ten dollars.

"Why three?"

"Because I didn't do any yesterday or the day before. She said work doesn't go away, and I have to catch up."

He sounded dangerously close to tears. That reminded Elizabeth that she had agreed to do something with him. Math would be better than a game.

"Would you like some help?"

Hope warred against disbelief in his eyes. Hope won, and he nodded. Elizabeth walked around the table and sat down.

"Where are you?"

He opened the book to page seven: ten addition problems. He had done three.

"This one's right." She carefully erased the other two answers. "Do this one again."

Paul counted on his fingers. "Eleven."

"Good. Write it down." He picked up the pencil and started to write the answer in the wrong place. "No. Over here."

Ponderously, they made their way down the page. Paul answered only four questions correctly on the first try. Page eight was a similar struggle. He sighed as he erased, but he kept doggedly at it. When he looked at page nine, he groaned.

Elizabeth's eyebrows drew together. There were only three questions on this page. "Just these and then you're done."

"But they're *word* problems."

Paul didn't know whether to add or subtract. He read fourteen and wrote forty-one. He omitted one number altogether. When at last he closed the book, Elizabeth became aware of having a headache.

"Are you *sure* all the answers are right?"

She nodded. Paul's shoulders relaxed and he grinned.

"Thanks, Elizabeth. A lot."

After dinner, Elizabeth exchanged her green shirt for a white one and added her cloak of invisibility. Twilight fell, rose colored and clear, and they set off for town. At the pavilion, people greeted Iron Woman warmly. The single exception was a large woman with tightly curled gray hair: Mrs. Davenport.

"Hello, Martha. So this is the new one, is it?"

*Unpleasant?! She's a serpent!*

Musicians began to tune instruments while people found places to sit on folding chairs and long benches. The band played six pieces. Then a dozen men in red bow ties sang patriotic songs. Three times the audience was invited to sing along.

Elizabeth smelled the ocean and began to feel itchy. The moon had risen. It was almost full and the area around the pavilion was bathed in gray light. The desire began as a tickle, rapidly became a hunger, and then turned into an overwhelming urge. She had to see the ocean by moonlight. Alone.

There was a break in the program. People stood up

to stretch and began to mill around. This was her chance.

"I have to go to the bathroom." Elizabeth pointed toward the theater, which had opened its doors for that purpose.

"Hurry," Iron Woman said. "The last part's the best."

Elizabeth nodded and wriggled into the crowd. Thirty feet away, she glanced back. A plump man with shiny dark hair had engaged Iron Woman's attention. She started to run.

On the beach, alone with the ocean, Elizabeth decided she understood the word "bliss."

"Elizabeth!"

From darkness into silvery light, Adam stormed toward her. His voice was a mixture of exasperation and relief and, a moment later, fury. "What are you *doing* down here?"

Sand glittered as it flew from his sneakers.

"Grandma's worried *sick!* Half the town is looking for you. What in hell made you take off like that?"

Adam's chest was heaving. Elizabeth chose not to look at his face.

"Go ahead!" He put his hands on his hips. "*Go* into your mute fish routine." He spat the words onto the sand. "It doesn't matter to me. But I can tell you right now, that isn't going to cut it with Grandma."

He turned and stamped away from her. "Come

*on!"* He pointed toward the road. "And hurry up about it. You've caused enough trouble as it is."

Elizabeth walked as quickly as she could, but Adam's legs were longer than hers and he was taking enormous, angry strides. She had to trot several times to keep up with him. She had thought they were headed back to the pavilion, but he marched straight home and up the driveway.

Andrew and Paul were standing on the lawn with several people whom she did not recognize. Sarah and Petey were huddled together on the swing. Abby stood on the steps. She couldn't see the others.

"Abby, go tell Grandma she's here," Adam barked. "Andrew, tell Grandma I've gone to look for Caro and Molly." He pointed an index finger at Elizabeth's chest and then at the grass. *"You* stay *put."*

Elizabeth took him at his word and stood still, her eyes on the ground. The screen door banged. Without moving, she glanced up. Iron Woman wavered for a moment at the edge of the porch. Then she hesitantly came down the steps and crossed the lawn. She looked Elizabeth up and down, as if to make certain her limbs were in place.

"Are you all right?" she finally asked. Her face was pinched and her voice sounded strangled.

"Yes."

Adam came up the driveway with Caroline and Molly. The telephone began to ring.

"I'll get it," Adam snapped.

When the ringing stopped, Iron Woman turned back to Elizabeth. "Please wait for me in the kitchen."

Back straight and eyes down, Elizabeth climbed the stairs. Adam had returned to the porch and stood glaring at her through narrow dark eyes. She walked around him and slipped through the door.

Footsteps echoed in the dining room and Elizabeth silently recited her litany.

*Do as you're told. Say as little as possible. Tell them what they want to hear and they'll leave you alone. Never let them see you cry. Never let them know what's important to you.*

Iron Woman stood in the doorway for a long moment and then abruptly crossed the room. She turned Elizabeth's chair to face the table squarely, pushed it in, and sat down across from her.

"I am so relieved that you are safe . . ." She dropped the words onto the table, one at a time. "And I am so *angry* . . ." She paused.

*To take a breath? For emphasis? To think?*

". . . that I don't know where to begin."

The telephone rang. Iron Woman got up to answer it.

"Hello?" Silence. "Yes. She's here, and she's safe. Thank you so much." She left her hand on the receiver for a moment and then came back to the table.

"Did you think, at *all*," she said slowly, "about what would happen when we realized that you were gone?"

Elizabeth shook her head. She *hadn't* thought about it. It had never crossed her mind.

"Did you think we wouldn't *notice?*"

*What am I supposed to say?*

"Do you have even the *faintest* idea . . ." Iron Woman's voice broke. Elizabeth's stomach twisted as she listened to Iron Woman take a deep, shuddering breath. ". . . how worried we were?" Shimmering gray eyes probed her face.

The telephone rang again. With a sigh, Iron Woman got to her feet.

"Hello? Yes, Adam found her. She's home, and she's all right. Thank you, Sam. And would you do me a favor? Would you call Evan and leave him that message? Thank you. Good night."

Iron Woman sat down again. "If it never occurred to you to consider the family's feelings or the trouble you might cause," she waved one hand toward the phone, "did it not occur to you that what you were doing was *dangerous?* That it might not be *safe* for an eleven-year-old girl to wander around by herself in the dark?" Her tone had grown harsh. "Do you have *anything* to say?"

Elizabeth shook her head.

"Not even, 'I'm sorry'?"

"I'm sorry."

Iron Woman stared at her. "But you're *not,* are you?" she said quietly. "I don't think you've *begun* to understand why it was so wrong to do what you did."

The clock tocked dully. A mechanical gurgle rose into a whine as one of the refrigerators began to drone. In the distance, explosive snaps were answered by an occasional *boom.*

"Then understand *this.*"

Elizabeth jumped.

"You will never, *ever* pull another stunt like that. You will *never* again go someplace without someone in this family knowing where you are." Her eyes flashed gray lightning. "Is that clear?"

Elizabeth nodded. The back of her neck tingled. Iron Woman had finished; she would be dismissed. Her feet slid toward her chair.

"There's something else, Elizabeth." Her voice was hard now.

*Like iron.*

"You lied to me."

*What?! Oh. When I said I was going to the bathroom.*

"You will not do so again." The words were ice. "Is *that* clear?"

Elizabeth suppressed a shudder and nodded.

Iron Woman carried the kettle to the sink and filled it. Metal scraped against metal as she set it on the burner. The gas hissed.

"Tomorrow, at breakfast, you will apologize to the

entire family." Iron Woman addressed the stove. "Go to bed now, and think about what you need to say."

Silently, Elizabeth slipped through the door and ran up the back stairs as fast as she could.

She would have found her way back. There wouldn't have been any trouble, or any neighbors bothered, or anything else, if Iron Woman hadn't gone off the deep end. Elizabeth hated her.

*I'm also afraid of her.*

She slammed her fist onto the bed.

*And I don't know* why.

Pink light flickered onto the window shade and a series of explosions ricocheted through the night. Elizabeth fought her way into her pajamas. She didn't care about having to apologize. She'd think of something to say and get through it. And she didn't much care that Adam despised her. In fact, it was a plus. The fewer people who talked to her, the fewer she had to answer.

Standing out of sight of the window, she lowered the shade and peeked around it. The oldest Sheridans were carrying the youngest ones into the house. She heard the ebb and flow of Iron Woman's voice and then heard feet on the stairs.

The blanket was over her head before the first person reached the landing.

# Chapter
## Nine

"Elizabeth?"

Breakfast was nearly over. Elizabeth glued her eyes to her watch and spoke in a carefully neutral tone. "I'm sorry about last night. I'm sorry I caused trouble, and I'm sorry you had to look for me. I won't do it again."

*Was that enough?*

"Thank you," Iron Woman said evenly. "We'll hold you to that promise." She stood up. "You may all be excused."

When the dining room was empty, Elizabeth went upstairs and looked out the window until the second floor was quiet. It was her morning to do the bathroom and she wanted to do it without being interrupted. As she scrubbed the sink, she reviewed her current situation.

Twenty-eight ocean days remained; that was good. She had infuriated Iron Woman; that was annoying. She had apologized to the family, and she had done something with Paul; those things were over. She would have to speak with Kevin and Karen; that was bad. She must not let herself be trapped again.

"Elizabeth?" Paul appeared to her left in the mirror. "Grandma said I can swim now if I do math before lunch." He twisted the doorknob back and forth. "Will you help me again?"

She studied the hot water faucet. She'd missed a spot.

"Just until I catch up," he said quickly. "Please?"

If she helped Paul, Iron Woman might stop telling her to join the others. And there was no doubt that Paul needed help. She nodded.

"Thanks!" He looked around the bathroom. "You almost done?"

Elizabeth nodded again and he took off down the hall. She polished the faucet, put the sponge under the sink, and followed him.

On the way to the beach Iron Woman answered a question from Petey, complimented Abby, reminded Molly about a telephone call, and laughed at something Caroline said. When they reached the sand, she waved to a friend, spoke briefly to Adam, and jogged into the water.

Elizabeth climbed her rock slowly. As she watched

the waves rock back and forth, she allowed the breeze to blow through her mind. Half an hour later, she felt ready to focus. She had spent three days watching and listening, and she was no further ahead. She decided not to spend any more time trying to *understand* Iron Woman. She would simply *avoid* her.

That, of course, was its own challenge. Iron Woman seemed to be everywhere, and the Sheridans did almost everything together.

It had been easier at Kevin and Karen's house. Including the bus ride, school had accounted for seven hours a day. It had been close to the end of the year, and Caroline had been preoccupied with her first set of high school exams. Paul had gotten pneumonia, and his parents had spent a great deal of time with him. When family life had threatened to overwhelm her, Elizabeth had said she had homework to do. She had been able to retreat to the quiet of her room and the solace of her ocean tape.

Kevin and Karen asked too many questions, and family dinner had been a nightly ordeal, but she had managed. Here, among *nine* Sheridans, without the respite of school or a room to herself, she felt surrounded and smothered. And Iron Woman was a constant threat.

*How can I stay away from her?*

The breeze had freshened and small whitecaps were visible away from the shore. Elizabeth wondered about the depth of the water beneath them and shuddered. It was easier to think about Iron Woman than it was to think about *that!*

She couldn't avoid meals, at least not very often, and she couldn't avoid kitchen jobs. Apart from those things, she would stay outside. There was the barn, and there was the side of the house opposite the clotheslines, the little alley under the dining-room window. No one else ever went there.

When Iron Woman was around, she would do what the others were doing. She'd hate it, but it would be better than dealing with her. Elizabeth sighed. Her plans were far from satisfactory, but she couldn't seem to do any better.

*Tweet! Tweet!* The beach was full of people and, for a moment, she could not distinguish the Sheridans from the rest of the crowd. *Tweet! Tweet!* One by one, Iron Woman's flock gathered around her. They huddled together for a moment and Elizabeth turned away.

It had been *so* peaceful last night . . .

As she climbed down the rocks, Elizabeth remembered that she had agreed to help Paul. She glanced at him. His hair glinted red in the sunlight and he was smiling to himself about something. Not math — she was certain of that. He *wasn't* stupid. How could simple arithmetic be so difficult for him?

*But he can swim.*

As they walked back to the house she puzzled about how very different one person could be from another.

The next several days were free of censure from Iron Woman, but her grandchildren were driving Elizabeth crazy. By now, they should have given up and begun to ignore her. That was the way it *always* happened. But the Sheridan kids continued to ask questions and invite her to play games. Elizabeth didn't know what was wrong with these people, but her neck had grown sore from shaking her head.

There was a reason no one spent time outside the dining-room windows: Elizabeth counted eighteen ant nests before being stung. Twice, she sat outside the barn. Once, she sat under the largest pine in the front yard. The rest of the time she sat on her bed, looking out of the window or pretending to read. She decided that Iron Woman was watching her less. If helping Paul was the reason, fifteen minutes of math before lunch was a small price to pay.

Elizabeth was conscious of, and grateful for, a respite from Sheridan noise. They weren't leaving for the beach for half an hour, and the porch was blessedly vacant.

It was too good to last. When the telephone rang, Elizabeth somehow knew it was Kevin or Karen. She didn't dare go as far as the barn, but she *might* not be seen under the tree. Silently, she sped across the grass. When Iron Woman came onto the porch, she knew she'd been right about the caller, and she knew she'd been spotted.

"Elizabeth, Karen's on the phone." Iron Woman peered over her glasses. "Paul's had his turn. Give Caroline five minutes, then come in."

Elizabeth glared at her watch. The second hand swept on and she forced herself to her feet.

"Here's Elizabeth. 'Bye." Caroline set the phone on the counter and darted down the stairs. The back door banged softly.

*Why is she crying?*

"Hello?"

Nine cheerful questions. Nine one-syllable answers.

"We miss you."

Karen gave the phone to Kevin and the process was repeated. He finally said good-bye and Elizabeth replaced the receiver. As she had known she would, she felt flustered and itchy and generally sullen.

*Why?*

She didn't know, and her irritation increased. Silently, she cursed Iron Woman.

"'That's what Mom said." A sob staggered through the window. "And I *have* tried." Caroline sobbed again. "For two and a half months!"

"I know you have, sweetheart. Come here."

Elizabeth slipped through the dining room.

Through the porch window, she listened to the throng gather. A few minutes later, Iron Woman stepped through the archway.

"Ready to go?"

"I don't feel very well. May I stay here?"

*She could probably take X rays with those eyes.*

Elizabeth quickly shifted her gaze to the fireplace. "I won't leave the house."

"Is that a promise?"

Elizabeth nodded.

"Then you may stay." Iron Woman looked back from the doorway. "I hope you feel better."

Elizabeth sat on her bed and listened to the wind wheeze through the screen. It was the first time she'd been alone in the house and she found the quiet disturbing. She hadn't lied to Iron Woman, either: she really didn't feel very well.

Restlessly, she pulled back the bedspread and tugged her pouch free from the pillowcase. The pouch was pale gray. On the bottom, in gold letters barely visible, were the words, "Genuine Imitation Leather" and "Made in Taiwan." On one side there were seventy-two very small holes where thirty-six plastic beads had been sewn.

Elizabeth slid open the drawstring and gently tipped four familiar objects onto the bedspread. In a scratched square box, blue sponges protected a sand dollar, a good-bye present from her second-grade teacher.

*What started it all . . .*

She rubbed her fingers across the indentations on the sand dollar's surface, put it back into its box, and gently closed the lid. She bypassed the next object: a rectangular box. It contained a cassette, and there was no tape player here. She recalled scratching the *Ocean Music* label from the tape as soon as she'd bought it.

She smoothed a wrinkle from her bookmark, a narrow strip of navy blue ribbon. *Prendre la mer!* it read, which meant something like "take the sea." The person who'd given it to her hadn't been sure. Perhaps it meant "take *to* the sea." Now that she'd seen the ocean, Elizabeth wished she knew which translation was correct. It mattered.

She picked up the last item and sighed — she might as well complete the ritual. She unfolded the picture frame and gazed down at the photograph of her mother and father. Sometimes she felt that, if she looked long enough, if she looked *hard* enough, her parents would speak to her. This afternoon they looked like cardboard cutouts. She snapped the frame closed, slipped everything back into the pouch, and put it back where she'd found it.

She leaned on the windowsill and looked up through the screen at the sky.

*What made Caroline cry?*

She had been crying before she left the kitchen. Had she been speaking to Kevin or Karen? "That's what Mom said." It must have been Karen. Why had

Karen made Caroline cry? And what had she been trying to do for two and a half months?

Her mind drifted. Kevin and Karen. The first time she'd met them they'd taken her to lunch and the zoo. The second time, Caroline and Paul had come, too, and they'd all seen an ice skating show. The third time, the day they'd asked her if she wanted to live with them, they'd told her about spending a month at the ocean. The following morning, the social worker had interviewed her and she had agreed to go.

A month. How many ocean days were left? She wouldn't count today. Dark clouds were gathering and the wind was blowing hard. It was unlikely they would swim after dinner.

*Twenty-seven days at the ocean.*

*Twenty-seven days with the Sheridans.*

*Everything costs.*

Mrs. Hartrick had been fond of saying that. It was true, she supposed. The moonlight trip to the beach had cost her a lecture and an apology. *Two* lectures, if she counted Adam's tirade. This afternoon, time away from Iron Woman had cost her time at the ocean. It annoyed her that she couldn't decide if the exchange had been worth it.

Elizabeth frowned at her watch: 4:17.

*It can't be that late.*

She checked her clock: 4:18.

The night before Elizabeth had left for the ocean, Kevin and Karen had surprised her with a watch that was waterproof, not just water-resistant, and a travel alarm with numerals that glowed in the dark. The gifts had made her extremely uncomfortable, but she had found them both very useful.

A gust of cold wind brought with it Sheridan noise. Elizabeth sighed. They were back almost an hour ahead of schedule.

As she waited in line to serve herself dinner, Elizabeth noted that Caroline was cheerfully bantering with Molly and Andrew.

*She seems O.K.*

Elizabeth reminded herself that it was her night for dishes. Then she turned her thoughts to the ocean. When it was her turn to tell her best, she chose the salad, passed her turn to Sarah, and took her mind back to the beach. When the table was clear, she went into the kitchen.

Iron Woman was putting things into the refrigerators. Elizabeth hoped she would leave, but she turned on a portable radio and began to mix batter for muffins. Elizabeth set herself the goal of being out of the kitchen in twenty minutes and went to work with a vengeance.

When the weather report began, Iron Woman turned up the volume. A cold front had moved in. Storm warnings had been issued and high winds were predicted.

"Tomorrow should be interesting." Iron Woman

put the muffins into the oven. She set the timer and carried the bowl and the whisk to the sink. "Would you mind doing these? I'd better get things off the clotheslines."

She went into the mudroom and then out the back door. Elizabeth finished the silverware, closed the dishwasher, and looked at her watch. Twenty minutes. Exactly. She sighed and reached for the mixing bowl. Another point for Iron Woman.

*Current score? Sheridan: four; Lawson: zero.*

# Chapter
## Ten

The weatherman had under-
estimated the effect of the
cold front. The temperature
dropped into the upper fifties
and stayed there. Wind and
rain hammered the house,
and the electricity went out
after breakfast.

Elizabeth longed to see what the ocean was doing,
but Iron Woman was adamant: it was too cold, too
wet, too windy, and power lines were down. No one
was to go out.

Elizabeth was determined to enjoy the storm, even
from inside the house. The problem was finding an
unoccupied window. Sarah and Abby were playing in
the bedroom, giggling and chattering at a level she
couldn't ignore. In the front room, Adam had built
Petey a miniature city out of cardboard and blocks.

The two of them were making zooming noises and crashing Petey's cars into make-believe buildings.

The kitchen was out: Iron Woman was there. The dining room was out: it was too close to the kitchen. The bathroom had seemed like a good bet, even if interruptions were to be expected. Unfortunately, Caroline and Molly had spread out every bit of makeup they owned.

Elizabeth wandered back to the front room. Adam was leaning over a book and Petey *zoomed* only inter-mittently. She settled herself by the window and watched such sky as she could see past the porch pillars. She had been there only minutes when a commotion erupted on the second floor.

Molly had found Andrew and Paul reading her diary. She screamed at them and cried. The boys each got a spanking, and everyone got a lunchtime lecture about the importance of respecting privacy. No going into each other's drawers, no reading anyone else's mail, no spying. No eavesdropping. Elizabeth was al-most certain Iron Woman was speaking in general terms. *Almost* certain, but not quite.

By one o'clock the storm had deteriorated into a steady, thrumming downpour. Adam offered to take Petey, Sarah, and Abby to the Tiny Theater to see *Snow White*. Iron Woman gave him a grateful look and money for tickets and popcorn. Four yellow slick-ers set off into the rain.

Under Iron Woman's watchful eye, Molly accepted apologies from Andrew and Paul. The three of them began a game of Monopoly and invited Elizabeth to play. She shook her head.

"Geez, Elizabeth!" Molly said crossly. "You never want to play *anything!*"

Iron Woman overheard her and called Elizabeth into the kitchen for a lecture about participating in family life. If she didn't want to play, she could help with dinner.

The gas was still on and they were having beef stew. Elizabeth scraped and diced one bag of carrots and two dozen potatoes. She dropped her last handful of vegetables into a bowl of water as the moviegoers stomped back into the mudroom. Abby and Petey scurried through the kitchen and out of sight. In quietly furious tones, Adam reported that Sarah had refused to walk with him and had almost been hit by a car. He went out to the barn, and Iron Woman took a tearful Sarah upstairs to be spanked. Elizabeth seized the opportunity to escape.

Wishing to avoid the front room, she walked around the house to the porch. For twenty minutes she listened to the rain and wondered why, no matter what, she never fit in.

When Abby burst through the door and slammed it behind her, Elizabeth almost fell off the railing. Caroline followed Abby out and spoke to her quietly. They went back inside, but it took Elizabeth fifteen minutes to regain her composure. She spent a few peaceful moments thinking about the ocean before Paul bellowed her name through the window. It was her turn to set the table.

Dinner had come to represent everything Elizabeth hated about family life in general, and family life at the Sheridans' in particular. She hated "No, thank you" servings. She hated elbows bumping her on both sides. She hated bests. She hated the noise when they *stopped* taking turns. She hated having to put down her fork every ten seconds in order to pass something to someone. She hated family jokes. It wasn't the jokes themselves—she probably wouldn't have found them funny. What she hated was not understanding things, not knowing what everyone else knew.

Elizabeth quietly slammed the last three spoons onto the table and wondered whether she should attempt her "not hungry" routine. She didn't feel up to putting on a first-class performance, and Iron Woman hadn't had the best of days. She decided against it. The power was still out, so she lit some candles and resigned herself to another forty-five-minute test of her endurance.

There was an unusual amount of whispering and giggling as plates were filled. When everyone had quieted down, Iron Woman suggested they try something different.

"Let's each tell *three* bests." Her eyes twinkled. "Whose turn is it to start?"

It was Adam's. "Playing cars with Petey, finishing *Watership Down*, and having the power out."

"Huh?" Paul wrinkled his nose.

Adam shrugged. "I like candles at dinner." He grinned and passed his turn to Abby.

There was a candle in front of Elizabeth and she lost herself in the flickering light. It was sort of like the ocean: always changing, but always the same.

A sudden burst of noise broke her concentration. There were shouts and groans amid laughter, and everyone was talking at once.

"You cheat, Grandma!" Paul hollered.

"Yeah, Grandma, no fair!" Abby chimed in.

"She can have nine bests if she wants to!" shouted Petey.

Iron Woman was grinning impishly. Finally, she held up her hands.

"All right, all right. I'll start over," she said. "Having all nine of my grandchildren *here* with me, safe and sound. Having the power out, because I like candles, too. And hearing the weatherman say it's going to be sunny and much warmer tomorrow."

Adam and Caroline laughed.

"I pass my turn to Andrew."

Elizabeth noticed a change in the sound of the rain against the side of the house. The wind must have picked up again. It had grown darker, and her candle seemed to shine more brightly. The flame drew her in and held her until somebody nudged her arm.

"It's your turn."

Caroline was smiling and Elizabeth wondered what new joke she had missed. She scowled at her plate. Why was everyone so quiet?

"We're doing *three* bests, remember?" Caroline prompted her.

"Carrots. And celery." Elizabeth spied part of a roll on Sarah's plate. "And rolls," she finished quickly.

The table exploded with laughter.

"I win!" Molly roared. "I called carrots."

"I win, too," argued Paul. "I said rolls!"

"Did anybody call celery?" Abby giggled.

The laughter dwindled to chuckles.

"May I be excused?" Elizabeth managed to keep her voice level.

"You may."

Elizabeth got to her feet and carefully slid her chair into place. The room had grown silent. A bit of gray light made its way through the front window and she found the stairs without bumping into anything. She climbed them noiselessly and shut the door to her room.

The light came on suddenly as power was restored. Savagely, she flicked the switch off, knelt by the window, and glowered into the water-soaked night.

When her crimson fury had faded to gray, Elizabeth gave serious consideration to running away. She could do it. The problem, of course, was where to go. In the city there were several options.

The fact that she was *not* in the city reminded her of the reason she had agreed to stay with Kevin and Karen Sheridan in the first place. There were twenty-six days left to spend in South Wales. No one was going to deprive her of those ocean days. She had waited too long and had put up with too much to allow that to happen.

There was a knock at the door. "Elizabeth? May I come in?"

A wave of pinpricks swept up her spine and into her neck.

*Why won't she leave me alone?*

The door opened. Iron Woman hesitated before sitting down on the bed. "Are you O.K.?"

"Yes."

*I'm just* fine. *Go away.*

Iron Woman leaned forward to rest her elbows on her knees. The damp darkness hid her expression. "Do you understand what happened at dinner?"

"No."

*And I don't care.*

"Let me try to explain. Telling bests helps us focus on positive things. It's a way to keep up with each other, a way to share."

*How stupid do you think I am?*

"So far, you haven't shared. You only pick something and say it so you can pass your turn."

Elizabeth's stomach twitched, but she managed to keep her arms and legs still.

"Tonight, the others made bets about which thing you'd choose. I didn't know about it, so when I asked everyone to tell three bests, they thought the whole thing was even funnier."

Elizabeth could hear laughter downstairs.

"They're frustrated because you won't let them in. They meant to tease, but I don't think they meant to hurt your feelings."

*They didn't. And they* won't.

"They're terrific people, Elizabeth. Every one of them." Iron Woman stood up. "I wish you'd give yourself a chance to find that out."

Elizabeth shuddered.

"Sleep tight." The door clicked closed.

*If only there had been some other way to get to the ocean!*

# Chapter
# Eleven

A piece of paper fluttered
onto the floor.

*What's that?*

Elizabeth had fallen
asleep quickly. She hadn't
heard Abby and Sarah come
up, and she hadn't seen them leave the note on her
bed. *We're sorry*, it read. It was signed by each of them:
Caroline, Molly, Adam, Petey (someone had printed
his name and he had traced the letters), Paul, Abby,
Sarah, and Andrew.

*Eight idiots.*

Seven. Petey was all right, and she was sure he
hadn't been part of the joke. Something tickled her
brain. What had he said? "She can have nine bests if
she wants to." The something pushed harder. "Having
all nine of my grandchildren here . . ."

Nine? Either Iron Woman couldn't count, or she

had included Elizabeth. Her stomach lurched and the note became a pile of confetti. She carried the pieces to the bathroom and dropped them into the toilet bowl. It was satisfying to pee on them and to watch them swirl out of sight.

As she brushed her teeth, the phrase "nine grandchildren" crept back into her mind. Why did those words make her feel as though there were spiders on her neck? She brushed harder as she looked out the window. The sun was not yet up, but the sky was clear. Her shoulders relaxed as she rinsed. It would be an ocean day.

The screen door creaked into the stillness. As she tied her sneakers, Elizabeth watched the sky. The sun rose on the opposite side of the house, and the color changes on this side were subtle and soothing. As violet dissolved into rose-tinted gray, the Sheridans began to bump their way toward daytime cacophony.

The door creaked again and Petey padded across the porch. His feet were bare, his hair was sleep tossed, and he had something in his hand.

"Hi, Turtle."

Her eyes narrowed. "Why did you call me that?"

"Grandma said you need time to come out of your shell. If I call you Turtle, I'll remember," he said with a four year old's logic and candor. He tipped his head. "I won't if you don't want me to."

Elizabeth studied him. Petey doesn't know *how* to tease, she decided. There was no malice in the name. "You can."

His face relaxed into its usual open expression. "Want to see something?"

She nodded.

He sat down and opened his fist. In his palm lay a metal cylinder of some sort. Two wires—one green, one red—protruded from a copper band. Elizabeth had no idea what she was looking at, but it was clearly a treasure. She tried to look appreciative.

Petey grinned. "Know what it is?"

She shook her head.

"Part of the guts of a *radio*," he said proudly.

"Breakfast is ready," Abby called.

"It's peaches!" Petey hopped off the swing. "And pancakes. C'mon, Turtle."

Elizabeth went.

When breakfast was over, Iron Woman called her into the front room. For the time being, she would be excused from having to tell her best at dinner on one condition: she must promise to *think* of one. Elizabeth agreed.

Iron Woman took the older girls into town to do errands. Elizabeth sat on the porch until the station wagon pulled in and Molly called to her to help carry the bags.

They had stopped at the post office. Four envelopes were addressed in Karen's handwriting, and one of them was handed to her. Aware that she was being watched, Elizabeth slid the letter into her pocket and began to put groceries away. When the counters were empty, the Sheridans went up to change.

Elizabeth frowned out the window. She didn't want the letter, and she certainly wasn't going to read it. She didn't want it *near* her, but she couldn't just throw it out. Someone was bound to see it when it came time to empty the garbage.

*The recycling box!*

The letter wouldn't be found, and it would be out of the house tomorrow. She slipped the envelope into a cereal carton and buried it four layers down. Her chest thudded as she made her way to the porch.

It was still windy, but the sky was pale blue and cloudless. Elizabeth spent a delightful morning on her rock. When she climbed down, she felt cleansed and renewed. The feeling lasted through her math session with Paul, through lunch, and through reading time. The throng chatted, quietly for a change, as it waited for Iron Woman.

The door opened only halfway.

"Adam, please go ahead. Elizabeth, I need to speak with you."

Her spirits plummeted as she followed Iron Woman toward the back of the house. The box and the letter were on the kitchen table.

*Even* garbage *isn't safe in this place!*

"Paul was looking for a coupon. He found your letter."

*Mail is personal!*

Elizabeth's neck and ears burned.

*It was addressed to* me!

"What you do with your mail is your decision, Elizabeth." Iron Woman spun the cereal carton into the recycling box. "But you need to think about something."

Elizabeth clenched her teeth and her fists.

"How would Karen feel if she knew? That you'd thrown out her letter without even bothering to open it?"

*She doesn't know. She won't know unless you tell her. And it's none of your business!*

Iron Woman's footsteps faded and the front door banged softly. Elizabeth stormed past the mudroom and slammed the back door as hard as she could.

*I didn't do anything wrong!*

Her head pounded wildly. The laundry flapped and the hose beckoned. Methodically, she soaked every piece of clothing and every towel on the line.

*And I'm not going to miss any more time at the ocean because of you, either.*

She carefully replaced the hose, marched to the beach, and climbed onto her rock.

Elizabeth would have liked to have seen Iron Woman's expression when she discovered that the clothes were wet, but it wasn't worth the risk of a confrontation. She was already lying on her bed when she remembered that Karen's letter was still on the kitchen table. She scowled. Iron Woman would have to deal with it. She had thrown it out once, and that was enough. Nevertheless, she was glad that her turn for Helping had been two nights ago.

Her ears caught a small sound and she glanced to her left. Petey was standing in the doorway. She stared at her pillow and hoped he'd go away.

"Hi, Turtle."

"Hi." She continued to stare.

"How come you're sad?"

Her eyes narrowed. "I'm not."

Petey nodded twice. "Yes, you are," he said softly.

He tiptoed down the hall and Elizabeth closed her eyes. Her throat felt full.

*He's right. How did he know?*

Elizabeth chose not to think about why. For once, she was glad when it was time for dinner. As they sat down she remembered that she'd been excused from telling her best.

*My best was soaking the laundry.*

Having kept her promise to think of a best, she retreated into herself. When dinner was over, she sat under the big pine until the bedroom light went on. Then she cautiously climbed the stairs. There was altogether too much noise coming from their room.

Caroline and Molly and Abby were organizing pillows and blankets. Sarah was nowhere in sight.

"Where have *you* been?" Caroline demanded. "It's almost time to go out."

*Go out?*

"To the *barn*." Molly spoke as though Elizabeth were hard of hearing or stupid or both.

Caroline glared at her. "You didn't listen to one single thing at dinner, did you?"

Molly snorted. "As if that's a change."

"Why don't you *explain* what we're doing, Molly?" Iron Woman spoke from the doorway. Sarah stood beside her, red eyed and sniffling.

"We're sleeping in the barn tonight," Molly said woodenly. "In the hay."

Caroline came to her rescue. "We usually sleep in our clothes. If you wear your green sweatshirt, one blanket will be enough."

Abby crossed the room and gave her sister a hug. "I'm sorry you can't, Sair."

"I hate stupid allergies!" Tears rolled down Sarah's cheeks.

*Why on earth would anyone want to sleep in a barn?*

"Aren't you guys *ready*?" Adam called from the stairs.

"Almost," Caroline hollered back. "Hurry up, Elizabeth. Get your stuff."

Elizabeth shook her head and Iron Woman turned toward her.

"You don't want to, Elizabeth?"

She looked at the floor and shook her head again.

"Figures." Molly said it quietly, but not quietly enough.

"Please wait for me in your room."

When Molly reached the hall, Iron Woman turned to Caroline. "You and Abby go ahead with the others. I'll be out to say good night in a few minutes." Arms full of bedding, they waddled through the door.

"Sarah, can you get the popsicles down by yourself?" Sarah nodded and grinned. "You may have a whole one. Please eat it on the porch, and please put the box back in the freezer."

Elizabeth's eyes darted back and forth across the floor. Somehow, once again, she was alone with Iron Woman. Was she in trouble for hosing the clothes, for leaving Karen's letter in the kitchen, or for some other reason?

*Does it matter?*

"Would you do me a favor?" Iron Woman asked slowly.

*Red alert!*

Every muscle in Elizabeth's body grew tight. What fundamental change in her personality would she be asked to make *now?*

"If you'd really rather sleep in the house, would you keep an eye on Sarah tonight? Put her to bed? I would like to sleep in the barn."

*This is not a question I can avoid answering.*

Still looking at the floor, Elizabeth nodded.

"Thank you. I'll explain to Sarah and come back up before I go out."

Elizabeth heard her knock on Molly's door. It was

quiet for a minute; then she heard two sets of footsteps go down the back stairs.

*I do not believe it. She's trapped me again!*

Elizabeth stood where she was, trying to figure out *how*. She was still standing there when Iron Woman returned with Sarah.

"I borrowed Paul's walkie-talkies. Sarah can listen to one ghost story and then she needs to go to sleep." Sarah smiled. Her lips were orange. "Run and brush your teeth." Her grandmother kissed her and Sarah scampered down the hall.

Iron Woman showed Elizabeth how the radio worked. "All set?" Elizabeth nodded. "Then we'll see you in the morning."

Sarah bounced into the room as the back door slammed. "Grandma says you and me are having a slumber party." She grinned.

The walkie-talkie crackled. "Spaceship Outrageous, calling Sarah! Come in, please!" Paul's voice was thin and metallic.

Sarah beamed. "Hi, Paul!" She spoke to every member of the family and then asked if Andrew would tell his red pirate story. Andrew thought that one might be a bit much for Petey at bedtime. How about the ghost and four horses?

In a different way, he was as good a storyteller as Molly. Where Molly used imitation to advantage, Andrew used descriptive detail. Elizabeth found herself listening intently and she was sorry when the story ended. The barn contingent chorused good night to them both, and Sarah turned off the machine.

"Can we leave the bathroom light on? And the door open a little?" Elizabeth was puzzled at being asked, but she saw no reason to say no. Sarah made those adjustments and climbed into bed.

"Good night, Elizabeth."

"Good night."

Ten minutes later, Sarah asked if she was awake. Would she read to her for a while? She brought Elizabeth a flashlight and the book she had been reading with Abby. They were up to chapter seven.

Elizabeth read that chapter and paused. Was Sarah asleep?

"You're a good reader, Elizabeth!" A moment of silence. "Just a little more? Please?"

She read chapter eight and turned off the flashlight. There was no response from the other side of the room. Another incomprehensible Sheridan day had come to an end.

# Chapter
# Twelve

Three full days passed without incident, and Elizabeth was keenly aware of the reprieve. Apart from thanking her for staying with Sarah, Iron Woman had not spoken to her. Elizabeth counted that as a blessing. She had spent her free time watching the ocean and trying not to think.

Sunday morning she awoke feeling tired and cross. After some reflection she realized that she was sick of looking over her shoulder, of never knowing when — or *why* — Iron Woman would attack.

At lunch, Mrs. Sheridan asked her a direct question. Elizabeth refused to look at her or to answer her. She was excused from the table and told to wait in her room. Now she had been summoned to the kitchen.

Iron Woman faced her with folded arms. "Most days, Elizabeth, you barely meet the minimum standards of civility." Twin thunderheads glowered at her. "At lunch you fell below them."

"*Grandma!*"

The scream belonged to Andrew, and there was terror in it. Iron Woman darted to the window.

"Andrew? What's wrong?"

"Grandma! In the barn! Paul's bleeding, and it's really bad."

Iron Woman thrust herself from the windowsill and dashed down the steps. "Get the first-aid kit! And ice!" The door banged.

Elizabeth pulled a bag of ice from the freezer. Then she realized that she had no idea what the first-aid kit looked like or where to find it. It was with profound relief that she heard footsteps.

"What was all that screaming about?" Caroline's voice was tight.

"Paul's hurt." Elizabeth pointed to the window. "Where do you keep the first-aid kit?"

Caroline pulled a white box from under the sink and, together, they ran to the barn.

Paul was lying on one hip, facing away from them. Iron Woman was kneeling next to him, her hands pressing down hard on a piece of blood-soaked cloth. Andrew stood behind them, silent and shirtless. Tears ran down his cheeks.

Caroline crouched down next to her brother. "Hey, Paul." She put one hand on his shoulder. "Didn't you know stunt men use *ketchup?*"

Paul managed a weak grin.

*He's awfully pale.*

"Caroline, dig out the butterfly bandages. And gauze and adhesive tape." Iron Woman looked up. "Elizabeth, would you bring me some cold water and a towel? A clean one."

Elizabeth dropped the ice next to Caroline and ran back to the house. She dashed up the stairs to the linen cupboard, grabbed a towel, and raced back to the kitchen.

*How* much *cold water?*

"What's going on?" Adam demanded from the dining-room doorway.

"Paul cut his leg." She spied a pitcher and hurried with it to the sink.

"Does Grandma know? Where are they?"

She nodded. "In the barn." Adam vanished.

Cold, at last! When the pitcher was full, Elizabeth tucked the towel under one arm and staggered her way across the lawn. Iron Woman thanked her without looking up. Then she patted her patient's back to get his attention.

"Paul, I have to clean it off a bit so I can see what I'm doing. I'm going to pour some water on it. Tell me to stop if it hurts too much."

"O.K.," he whispered apprehensively.

*He's being awfully brave.*

"I'll start at your ankle."

Paul's leg twitched. Iron Woman waited a moment before slowly pouring water near the wound. Cautiously, she lifted the cloth to reveal a large j-shaped cut and shifted the stream to flow over it. Paul hunched his shoulders, but he didn't ask her to stop. When the cut started to bleed again, she pressed the towel over it.

"Stitches for sure, Paul."

He groaned.

"And I'm afraid you'll need a tetanus shot, too." She continued to press on the towel. "But you *will* live to tell the tale."

*She just hugged him with her voice!*

Elizabeth was certain of it.

*How did she do that?*

"Do you want me to take him to the hospital?"

"Thank you, Adam, but they won't let a minor sign the consent forms." She peeked under the towel and pressed down again. "Speaking of consents, please don't let me leave without the Just-in-Case folder."

Three or four minutes later, Iron Woman lifted the towel and nodded.

"O.K., nurse." She gave Caroline a quick smile. "Hand me those butterflies. One at a time, please."

The bandages looked like tiny beige bridges across a maroon river.

"Wrapping this will be a whole lot easier if you're

standing up, Paul. Adam and Caroline, will you help him?" she said. "And we'd better splint it. There might be a fracture in there. Andrew, will you find something?"

Adam gave Paul a piggyback ride to the car. Elizabeth and Caroline folded down the backseat and Paul crawled in through the rear door. Andrew handed him a pillow and placed his grandmother's wallet and the Just-in-Case folder on the front seat. Iron Woman put her arm around his shoulders and whispered something. Andrew smiled very briefly; then his eyes filled again. She kissed his cheek and climbed into the car.

"Not your day, Paul." She smiled into the rearview mirror. "This ambulance doesn't have a siren."

He grinned back. "Let's *get* one!"

She turned the station wagon around and called out the window.

"Adam and Caroline, will you hold things to-gether? Find the others and explain what happened. For the sake of my peace of mind, please don't go swimming until we get back. My nerves are *not* what they were." She crossed her eyes and they laughed.

"We promise." Adam raised his right hand.

"Don't worry," Caroline added.

"Thank you."

*She just hugged* them . . .

Elizabeth followed the car with her eyes until it disappeared.

Caroline and Adam called everyone onto the porch. They explained what happened. And they answered questions: Was Paul going to die? Would the doctors cut off his leg? What had it looked like? Had Paul cried? How many shots would he get? In his arm or his bottom? Why was Andrew so sad? Would they use a sewing machine to stitch up his leg? Why had Grandma said not to swim? When would they be home?

When the questions had been exhausted, the older kids began to construct an obstacle course that included the sprinkler. In the course of the afternoon, it grew to cover the lawn.

Elizabeth wandered toward the back of the house. Out of habit, she checked the job list. Under her name, across from today's date, was written, *Helping*.

Iron Woman wasn't here to be helped, but . . . at the Wilsons', Elizabeth had seen a cooking show that emphasized variety: food groups, colors, textures, tastes. She had been intrigued by the possible combinations—permutations, they were called. Planning a meal was like solving a math problem.

From the freezer door, Paul's skull glowered at her. She glowered back.

*I'm here on legitimate business.*

*Salad.* Lots to pick from: lettuce, spinach, cucumbers, two kinds of peppers. *Main dish.* Spareribs? That would involve the barbecue, and Adam. What else was there? Cheese. There was plenty of Swiss and plenty of cheddar. She looked at the counter. The pile of stale bread was still there. She'd make cheese pie. If they didn't like it, at least they wouldn't starve. *To go with it?* Apples, and a whole jar of celery sticks, already cut. *Dessert?* Iron Woman had baked and the cookie jar was full.

Satisfied, Elizabeth buttered the largest baking pan she could find. She layered the bread and the cheese, poured a milk-and-egg mixture over the top, and put it into the oven. She was washing lettuce when the telephone rang.

Hoping that someone else would answer it, she waited. Six rings. Seven. Apparently, she was alone in the house. Eight. The answering machine kicked in. After the recorded message, Iron Woman spoke.

"Hi, everyone. It's ten after five and we're still at the hospital. Paul's all stitched up, and he's going to be fine, but they want to take an X ray. If we're not back by six, please order pizza. There's money in the drawer of the front-hall table." There was a brief pause. "We'll be home as soon as we can." The machine clicked and whirred.

*Too late.*

Elizabeth finished the salad and tossed the apple slices with brown sugar and lemon juice. Was there enough to eat? She rummaged through the cupboard. Cranberry bread could bake at the same temperature as cheese pie. She quickly stirred the batter and put it into the oven. Had she forgotten anything?

Strictly speaking, cooking dishes were the responsibility of the after-dinner team, but Elizabeth didn't want to leave any of *her* mess in *Iron Woman's* kitchen. After she washed and dried every dish she had used, she scrubbed the counters.

"Something smells good!" Caroline stepped into the kitchen. "Where's Grandma? And Paul?" She looked around. "Aren't they back yet?"

Elizabeth shook her head and pointed to the answering machine. The green light was blinking. Caroline played the message and waved her hand at the table.

"*You* did all this?"

Elizabeth shrugged. "I'd already started."

She took the cheese pie from the oven and went back for the bread. Caroline watched her in fascinated silence. The rest of the family began to shout and bang its way into the house. One by one, they made their way to the kitchen.

Caroline pulled herself together. Grandma and Paul weren't home yet, Elizabeth had made dinner, and whose turn was it to set the table? Routine took over and the kitchen was soon empty of people and food.

"Hey! Julia Child!" Adam called. "We're waiting for you."

Suddenly, she didn't want to eat.

"Elizabeth?"

"Go ahead," she called back. "I'm not hungry."
She tiptoed across the kitchen and up the back stairs.

Bright amber sunlight streamed through her
window. She lowered the shade until only inches of
screen were visible and watched the station wagon
pull into the driveway. Paul was limping badly, but he
was babbling brightly. Something he said made Iron
Woman laugh. Uneven steps crossed the porch. The
door banged, and the first floor was filled with cheers
and applause.

Elizabeth's stomach growled. She'd been excused
from lunch before she'd even started her sandwich,
and the cheese pie *had* smelled good. She flopped
onto her bed and counted the ocean days that remained. With luck, there would be an average of four
hours each day at the beach. She amused herself by
converting the hours into minutes.

A knock made her jump. The door opened a crack
and she sat up quickly.

"Hello."

*Iron Woman. Of course.*

"They said you weren't hungry. I wanted to be
sure you're not sick."

"I'm not."

Iron Woman felt Elizabeth's forehead with the
back of her hand. "No fever."

*I said I wasn't sick.*

"You made a beautiful dinner. I'm very impressed."

*No big deal.*

"Thank you for doing it. And for leaving the kitchen cleaner than you found it."

*"Leave it better than you find it." Another Sheridanism.*

Elizabeth wished she'd left everything in the sink. She wished she hadn't *made* dinner. She wished Iron Woman would go away.

"We're going for an after-dinner swim. Would you like to come?"

*Another sixty minutes to add to the total. Maybe ninety!*

Elizabeth shook her head.

*Not if it means saying yes to you.*

"Sure?"

She nodded.

"Caroline's downstairs with Paul. We'll be back in an hour or so." She went out, leaving the door open.

When she was certain that Iron Woman had gone downstairs, Elizabeth closed the door and tried to distract herself with a book. Half an hour later, she couldn't stand it any longer. Her head hurt. She *had* to get something to eat. Maybe she could sneak into the kitchen, and out again, without having Caroline notice.

She eased open the door and almost stepped on a tray. A red-and-white napkin covered a plate filled with the dinner she'd made. There were also two cookies, a glass of milk, and a note in Iron Woman's neat script: *In case you feel better* was all it said.

Elizabeth was furious at herself that she hadn't heard Iron Woman in the hall. She'd leave the tray right where it was. She didn't want it! She *didn't,* but she couldn't help herself. In four minutes, it was gone. All of it.

As she rinsed the dishes in the bathroom sink, she thought about what Iron Woman had said. "I'm very impressed," had sounded genuine.

*There's lots you don't know about me.*

That highly satisfying thought was followed by a disconcerting one.

*You know something about me that you didn't know yesterday.*

Elizabeth scowled. As she shook the water from the silverware, she renewed her determination to remain on her guard whenever Iron Woman was near.

# Chapter
# Thirteen

Breakfast was ugly. Caroline would not shut up about dinner.

"Grandma's waited *years* for an heir to her culinary genius," she said with a grin. "And she's suffered horribly. Except for the grill, Adam hates to cook. Molly and I are all thumbs, and Andrew eats the ingredients. Good thing you came along!"

"Yeah, Elizabeth," piped Sarah. "When *they* cook," she pointed to Adam and Caroline, "it's sandwiches." She bounced. "*You* cook like *Grandma!*"

Elizabeth's temples pounded.

"Is today when we see the sharks?" Petey's voice was louder than usual.

"It certainly is." Iron Woman smiled at him and

checked her watch. "We leave for the aquarium in half an hour, so everyone hustle with chores!"

Last bites were hurriedly consumed, plates clattered in the kitchen, and happy anticipation filled the house.

Elizabeth swept the porch with savage strokes. She hadn't known that today—what should have been an *ocean* day—would be wasted on some stupid trip. Iron Woman would never let her stay behind by herself. She knew better than to ask.

Paul had asked Adam how long the drive would be. An *hour*. Elizabeth swept harder. If she had known that, she wouldn't have eaten anything. Now she'd probably throw up. She stomped onto the stairs and swiped the broom at them viciously.

"Turtle?" Petey was standing next to the swing. "How come you're mad?"

"Because!" she snapped, and immediately felt worse.

*It's not his fault we're going.*

"Sorry," she muttered as she climbed the stairs.

"It's what Sarah said, isn't it?" Petey's sapphire eyes clouded over.

*What is this kid, a miniature psychologist? What does he know about why I'm mad?*

"Leave me alone!" Elizabeth stomped into the house, slammed the door, and froze. Iron Woman had been walking right toward her. Now she stopped and slowly raised one eyebrow.

*On guard!*

Elizabeth carried the broom to the closet, quietly closed the door, and turned toward the stairs.

"It's time to go." Iron Woman's voice was even, but it contained a warning.

"I need to use the bathroom."

"Hurry, please."

*She doesn't believe me.*

Elizabeth stepped onto the landing.

*So what?*

There was a line outside the bathroom and she went into her room to wait. Iron Woman's voice drifted through the window. Elizabeth couldn't make out the words, but her inflection was soothing.

*Damn it!*

When the second floor was quiet, she flushed the toilet, put on her cloak of invisibility, and went down the stairs.

". . . highway driving, Adam. I want you to take the car you already know."

The throng was assembled between Mrs. Sheridan's gray station wagon and a green one that had apparently been borrowed for the day. By name, Iron Woman assigned people to cars. Petey would ride with his grandmother. Elizabeth would go with Adam.

The trip was every bit as awful as she had anticipated: Sheridan noise and rancid stomach. By sheer force of will, she managed not to throw up. Iron

Woman and Adam found parking spaces next to each other and the group crossed the parking lot in a single swarm. Because there were ten of them, they qualified for a special discount.

"How about that?" Adam raised his arms to encompass the group. "We're a *field trip!*" The Sheridans burst into laughter.

*Why do they think that's funny?*

Iron Woman spoke to the man behind the counter and a wheelchair appeared.

"It's a big building, Paul. Your leg might start to ache."

"Cool!" Paul beamed. "Thanks!" He dropped onto the seat and immediately began to figure out how to set the brake.

"Can I drive?" Andrew's hands were already on the back of the chair.

His grandmother nodded. "You two are buddies. The rest of us, younger with older: Petey with me, Sarah with Adam, Abby with Caroline, Elizabeth with Molly."

Iron Woman led them through the double doors that separated the lobby from the exhibit area. Elizabeth had never been to an aquarium. She supposed there would be tanks with fish in them. She didn't know what else to expect.

There *were* fish. *Thousands* of them.

Streamlined fish swam in schools, pulsing and

darting, flashing silver as they changed direction. There were solitary snakelike fish whose fins rippled ominously as they hovered above the sand. There were fish so flat they disappeared as they swam away. There were fish so brightly colored that it was hard to believe they were fish at all. A scorpionfish lurked upon the ocean bottom. The lionfish looked like a striped feather duster, the anglerfish like a Halloween mask, and the hatchetfish as though it had been misassembled.

And there were other creatures. An octopus held them fascinated as it stuck its tentacles to the glass. In another tank, something called a cleaner fish darted in and out of the mouth of a moray eel. They saw pink squid and golden crinoids and lime green sponges, and tiny jellyfish that were nearly invisible.

There were seaweeds and corals and kelps, and sea fans and barnacles. They saw sea horses of all different sizes, and animals whose shells they collected: scallops and moon snails and whelks. There were horseshoe crabs and hermit crabs and a wormlike creature that could open clam shells. There were videotapes of creatures too small to see. One kind of plankton looked like glass ornaments. Another kind looked like miniature shrimp.

*It all lives in the ocean.*

They were eating lunch in a food court. Mindful of the drive still ahead, Elizabeth had limited her order to a small cola. It remained untouched on the table. The variety of what she had seen, the beauty of it, the *complexity* of it, left her stunned.

"Hey, ozone woman!" Molly waved a hand in front of Elizabeth's face. "We're leaving."

They weren't going home. A water show was scheduled to begin at one o'clock and Iron Woman had been persuaded to let them see it. An enormous kidney-shaped pool was filled with turquoise water. Six men and women in black wet suits stood along its edge. The announcer's voice blared and the show began. For half an hour, killer whales and dolphins swam through things, jumped over things, allowed the wet suits to ride them, and splashed the audience on command.

Elizabeth was appalled.

As they crossed the parking lot, she tried to reconcile the two aquariums she had seen. The first had seemed to respect the ocean's inhabitants; the second, to denigrate them. She thought about it all the way home, while she waited for the Sheridans to change, and during the walk to the beach.

Laughing, the Sheridans ran into the water. Deep in thought, Elizabeth climbed her rock to look at it.

# Chapter Fourteen

*Just one more minute . . .*

Elizabeth hurried onto the sand. She had made it through the entire evening and breakfast without having to speak. She scaled her rock, sat down, and slowly exhaled. She was safe.

*. . . at least until lunch.*

She spent a fragmented morning trying to imagine the aquarium's killer whales swimming in the ocean, wishing she were someone else, and deciding that the Sheridans were a two-legged school of fish. Her head hurt and she was glad when it was time to go home.

They had almost reached the driveway when Iron Woman came up behind her.

"Do you know the meaning of the word "empathy," Elizabeth?"

She shook her head.

Iron Woman glanced at her briefly. "I didn't think so." Without another word, she walked toward the clotheslines.

*What was that all about?*

The question nettled her during lunch and through reading time. When Iron Woman drove into town, Elizabeth went into the front room and opened the dictionary. She read the definition two times, climbed the stairs, and looked out the window.

Caroline and Petey ambled down the driveway. A few minutes later, Molly took a bicycle from the shed and rode off. At the side of the house, Adam began to referee some sort of game. Elizabeth decided she needed the quiet of the barn and went out. An hour later, she walked back to the house and read the definition again: "experiencing the feelings or thoughts of another."

Someone trotted up the steps to the porch. "Hey, Caro! What's up?"

"You won't believe this, Molly. Petey got spanked."

"*Petey?!* What *for?*"

Caroline giggled. "Throwing sand at Mrs. Davenport."

Molly laughed out loud. "Good for him! I hate that stuck-up old hag. What happened?"

Caroline giggled again. "Petey and I went to mail letters, and we were walking back. Davenport was

standing in her front yard, near the fence, talking to—
what's her name? The lady who always wears a cardi-
gan, even when it's ninety."

"Mrs. Terhune," prompted Molly.

"That's it, Mrs. Terhune," said Caroline. "Anyhow,
when we walked by, Davenport said something like,
'How's that new sister of yours?' and I said, 'Fine,
thanks,' and kept going."

"*Then* what?" Molly demanded.

"Then she turned to Mrs. Terhune and wiggled
her shoulders around in that stupid way she does, and
she said really loudly, 'That *Elizabeth* was a mistake.'"

Caroline started to laugh. "Then Petey grabbed a
pile of wet sand from in front of her fence and threw
it at her, right at her stomach, and it *stuck*. Then he
yelled, '*She's* not a mistake, *you* are!' and took off."

The two of them dissolved into laughter.

"I wish I'd been there," Molly finally gasped.

"I wish we had it on tape," snickered Caroline.
"Especially the expression on her face!"

Molly laughed again until she couldn't catch her
breath.

"By the time we got home, Davenport had
Grandma on the phone. When Grandma got off,
she asked me what really happened."

The laughter had gone out of Caroline's voice
and Elizabeth had to strain to hear what she was
saying.

"So I told her, and she looked daggers at Petey and asked me to be excused."

"Poor kid," said Molly. "And on account of *Davenport.*"

"Yeah," Caroline agreed. "Grandma took him off to apologize just before you got home."

Elizabeth was more disturbed than she cared to admit. Yesterday, she had yelled at Petey. She had told him to leave her alone and she hadn't spoken to him since. In *spite* of that, he had defended her to the serpent lady. And on *top* of it, Iron Woman had spanked him.

*Not a lot of fairness in this picture.*

She went into the kitchen and looked out the window. Petey was lying on his stomach near the picnic table. She slipped out the back door and sat down.

"Hi."

"Hi." His blue eyes flickered toward her and back to the red jeep in his hand.

"I'm sorry you got spanked."

He nodded. "Four times." He continued to push the jeep through the grass for a moment. Then he squinted up at her. "How did you know?"

"I heard Caroline tell Molly."

"Oh." He ran the jeep back and forth over her sneakers for several minutes before flipping it onto its side. "She made me tell sorry." Damp lashes framed shimmering eyes. "And I'm *not.*"

He put his forehead down on his arms.

Somewhere nearby, a lawn mower coughed into action. A dragonfly darted into view and came to rest on the picnic table. It lost its iridescence and then its color as it flew toward the barn. A gentle breeze stirred Petey's hair.

"When you're on the rock, can you see forever?"

*Where does he get these questions?*

Elizabeth shook her head.

*What an image, though.*

She looked at him and thought about it.

*Maybe I can.*

Tentatively, she nodded. "Sort of. Sometimes."

They sat without speaking until Adam called Petey to change.

"Walk with me, Turtle?"

Elizabeth's eyebrows drew together. Petey usually walked with his grandmother. She remembered why he wouldn't want to, and nodded.

He chattered to her about a slug he had found when he'd lifted a rock. Looking at it had made him feel shivery, the way he felt when he came out of the ocean. The slug had looked wet. He had wanted to touch it, but he hadn't wanted to hurt it. He didn't think it had liked the sunshine, but he hadn't seen any eyes. Did slugs have eyes? They didn't have feet. Did they have feelings, like people?

Elizabeth was relieved when they reached the sand and Andrew offered to take him swimming. She

climbed her rock slowly, her attention divided between the ocean and Petey. Andrew carried him into
the waves and stood in one place, bobbing a little
when a crest passed them. They stayed there almost
twenty minutes. Once, very briefly, Petey looked over
his brother's shoulder at his grandmother.

When Andrew brought him back to the water's
edge, Petey began to dig in the sand. Abby crouched
down beside him. He shook his head, and she followed Sarah into the water. Petey dug a second hole.
When his grandmother got up to swim, he watched
her. When she came out of the water, he started to
dig a canal.

Iron Woman sat down about ten feet away from
him. Petey carried a bucket into the waves and filled
it. He watched the water flow from one hole into the
other, knelt down, and began a third hole.

Crablike, Iron Woman scooted toward him a few
feet. Petey glanced at her and went back to digging.
Two minutes later, she did it again. He didn't look at
her, but he dug faster. When she did it a third time,
Elizabeth could tell that Petey was trying hard not to
smile. Iron Woman said something and he laughed.
She opened her arms and he launched himself at
her. They hugged each other for four minutes and
fourteen seconds. Then they went into the water
together.

By the time she climbed down from her rock,
Elizabeth had come to the conclusion that the

Sheridans and she were not of the same biological species.

That notion was reinforced when she refused to play volleyball and Caroline started to cry. Adam gave Elizabeth a glacial look, put his arm around Caroline's shoulders, and walked her around the side of the house. Twenty seconds later, Elizabeth locked the bathroom door. Through the window she heard Caroline say, "Shut *up*, Adam!" and laugh.

Elizabeth put her hands over her ears. By the time she took them away, the volleyball game had begun. She closed the window against Sheridan vitality and sat on the edge of the tub. She did not move a muscle when dinner was called or when Andrew delivered Iron Woman's message that attendance at meals was not optional. When he left, Elizabeth beat a hasty retreat to her bed.

Adult footsteps came down the hall and she felt her throat narrow. She was too close to tears to risk open warfare. Elizabeth scurried off her bed and ran down the stairs before Iron Woman had a chance to speak.

Dinner was full of tension. Afterwards, Elizabeth sat on the porch and counted the minutes until it was time to go up.

*The only time I'm safe in this house is when I'm asleep.*

She brushed her teeth, put on her pajamas, and crawled into bed. Her foot touched something. She scrambled onto her pillow and threw back the covers.

A *snake!*

"*Auk! Auuuukkk!*"

Her scream echoed as bare feet charged down the hall.

"Who yelled?" Caroline looked at Elizabeth, at the bed, at Abby and Sarah. She raised her eyebrows. Molly, then Andrew, and then Paul swarmed into the room.

"Is someone hurt?" Footsteps came up the stairs quickly.

"No," Caroline called.

Iron Woman came through the door. She glanced at Elizabeth, still trembling in the corner. Then she walked to the bed and picked up the snake.

*It's fake. Rubber, not real.*

"Paul?" she asked in an ominous tone.

"I didn't do it, Grandma! Honest!"

"I did it." Abby's voice was filled with regret.

"How'd you get my snake?" Paul demanded.

"I was putting clean shirts in your drawer and I saw it. So I borrowed it." Abby looked at her grandmother. "I thought she'd *see* it. I didn't think she'd get in on *top* of it."

Iron Woman gazed at her for a moment and then lifted her chin toward the hall. Head down, Abby crossed the room. "I'm sorry," she mumbled and ducked through the crowd.

"All right, everybody. Time for bed." Iron Woman held the snake toward its owner. "I apologize for jumping to conclusions, Paul."

He gave her a quick half-smile. "That's O.K."

Iron Woman turned toward Elizabeth. "Are you all right?"

She nodded. Iron Woman left the room, closing the door behind her. With sorrowful eyes, Sarah watched Elizabeth remake her bed.

*I wish I hadn't screamed.*

Elizabeth finished tucking in her blanket, climbed into bed, and hugged her knees. The door opened.

"I'm sorry, Elizabeth." Abby's voice was thick. "I didn't mean to scare you that bad. It was supposed to be a joke." A tear slid down one cheek. "If you want, I'll do your chores tomorrow to make it up to you."

Elizabeth shook her head and Abby faced her grandmother with brimming eyes.

"The chores are your choice, Elizabeth, but it would help Abby a lot right now if you would accept her apology."

*Tell them what they want to hear.*

"I accept your apology."

Abby sniffed once and sighed.

"All right, Abby. Hop into bed."

Iron Woman tucked in Sarah's blanket and kissed her. She did the same for Abby and turned out the light. "Fresh start tomorrow," she said. "Sleep tight." The door closed.

*What did she mean? How could accepting her apology help Abby?*

Elizabeth pressed her burning eyes into her pillow. *Not just different species. Different kingdoms.*

# Chapter
# Fifteen

 Over the next three days, Elizabeth's outlook matched the weather. Thursday was cool and overcast. Friday was cold and rainy. Saturday was cloudy and muggy, and she felt listlessly out of sorts. They'd gone to the ocean twice and she hadn't enjoyed it either time. After lunch, Adam had gone to bed with the flu. She slumped onto the swing wondering if she had it, too.

"Elizabeth!" Paul called. "Grandma wants you in the kitchen."

Elizabeth searched her mind. As far as she *knew* she hadn't done anything wrong, but that was no guarantee she wasn't in trouble.

"Hi, Turtle!" Petey said brightly. He was peeling shells from hard-boiled eggs.

"Hi."

A steaming mug sat on the stove. Iron Woman added a tea bag and some sugar, put the mug on a plate, and held it toward Elizabeth.

"Would you please take this up to Adam? It's too hot for Petey to carry."

Elizabeth tiptoed up the stairs to the Crow's Nest.

*Thank goodness. He's asleep.*

Adam's hair was scribbled and his face was very pale.

*He looks younger with his eyes closed.*

She glanced around her. There were windows in the triangular walls that faced east and west. Adam and Petey could watch the sun rise *and* set. Their room was remarkably neat—nothing at all like the room Paul shared with Andrew. She set the tea next to an empty bowl on the floor, crept back to the stairs, and looked over her shoulder. She hadn't awakened him.

Elizabeth was tired of thinking. She distracted herself by listening to the conversation at dinner, most of which centered on plans for the evening. The older girls had been invited to a party at the twins' house. After two phone calls and a minor inquisition, Iron Woman had given them permission to go. Caroline and Molly chattered happily at the prospect. The party was only three blocks away and they were going to walk. They would leave at ten minutes to eight and they were to be home at ten.

Petey wanted to sleep in the Crow's Nest in case Adam needed him. Iron Woman smiled, but said she didn't want him to catch Adam's flu. Paul asked if they could have a slumber party on the floor in his and Andrew's room. Iron Woman said that if they could *find* the floor, the answer would be yes, and she would make popcorn. Andrew and Paul grinned, and Petey bounced in his chair.

Abby and Sarah had asked Iron Woman to make some doll clothes. Tonight would be a good night. As soon as the dishes were done, they would begin. For some reason, one she chose not to explore, Elizabeth did not want to stay upstairs by herself. She took a book down to the porch and listened through the window while the girls talked and Iron Woman sewed.

Elizabeth sat up slowly. The toilet had flushed and water was running. She crawled out of bed, cracked open the door, and watched Adam stagger across the hall. She listened to him climb the stairs. Iron Woman's door was open and her room was dark, but the lights in the front room were on. As quietly as she could, she made her way down. The step above the landing creaked and Iron Woman looked up with a start.

"I think Adam threw up," Elizabeth whispered. "He looked really awful."

"Thank you for coming to tell me." Iron Woman followed her back to the second floor, murmured

"Good night," and climbed the steps to the Crow's Nest.

Elizabeth closed the bedroom door softly.

*Why is she still in her clothes?*

It was sticky and hot. Elizabeth crept to the window and raised the shade. The air outside felt just as heavy as the air in her room. The sky was a uniform gray and the usual night noises sounded muffled. Iron Woman tiptoed back down the stairs.

*Why was she just sitting there? She* never *just sits.*

There were mumbled voices at the end of the driveway. Her eyes widened.

*Caroline and Molly?*

Her clock read 11:16. The screen door creaked. The girls crossed the lawn and stood at the bottom of the steps to the porch.

"Are you two all right?"

"Yes." Caroline glanced at Molly and back to her grandmother. "We're sorry we're late."

"I am much too angry right now to listen to anything you have to say. We'll start with the fact that you are both grounded until your parents arrive. The rest of it will keep until morning. Go to bed. *Immediately.*"

Elizabeth lowered the shade. The inside door stuck in humid weather. As she got back into bed, she heard Iron Woman force it closed.

Elizabeth was astonished to see Adam in the dining room the next day. He had circles under his eyes and he still looked pale, but he filled his plate and told Petey he was sorry he'd missed the slumber party.

Breakfast was quiet and uncomfortable. The question, "Where are Caroline and Molly?" bounced from eye to eye. When the last of the eggs had disappeared, Iron Woman spoke.

"Caroline and Molly are on the porch. They made some mistakes last night, and they're working them out. I want the rest of you to leave them alone until they are finished." She looked at each of them. "Understood?"

There were worried nods around the table.

It was Molly's turn to get groceries and Iron Woman asked Elizabeth to go in her place. Adam seemed unaware of her presence beside him in the car.

When they returned, Iron Woman explained that she had allowed Andrew to take the little ones to the beach as long as no one went into the water until Adam arrived. Was he feeling well enough? He nodded and went up to change.

She was sorry to have to ask, but it was Caroline's turn to unpack. Would Elizabeth please put the cold food away?

Elizabeth did so and then went out the back door. As she passed the corner of the house, she glanced sideways. At opposite ends of the porch, Caroline and Molly were hunched over pads of yellow paper. She hurried down the driveway.

The ocean was monotonous and the seagulls quarreled loudly. Elizabeth turned to find the others. Andrew was wading along the beach. Abby and Sarah were standing knee deep in water. Petey and Paul were digging paths between mounds of sand. The plastic that covered Paul's bandage gleamed dully. Motionless, Adam sat by himself.

At lunchtime, the swimmers walked around back to hang up their towels. Thinking the porch was empty, Elizabeth climbed the stairs. Only after she reached the top step did she realized that Caroline was lying on the swing. She was writing.

*Still? Again?*

Molly wasn't there. Caroline did not look up, and Elizabeth quickly slipped through the door. As Elizabeth entered the kitchen, Iron Woman came up the steps from the mudroom.

*She's unhappy and worried.*

Elizabeth was surprised at her certainty and disconcerted by having made the observation. She repressed a shudder.

"I'm sorry to have to ask you again, Elizabeth, but would you help with lunch?" Iron Woman pointed to the table. On it lay two loaves of bread, a jar of peanut butter, and three kinds of jam. "Half grape, half strawberry, and a peach one for Petey, please."

Elizabeth had spread sixteen slices of bread with peanut butter and eight with grape jelly before Iron Woman returned. Elizabeth watched her drain carrots,

pour milk, and wash fruit. She did it all with effi-
ciency, but she seemed to lack energy. Or interest,
or something.

Elizabeth began to cut the sandwiches. A moment
later, Caroline came into the room and tentatively offered her grandmother an envelope. It was addressed
to Kevin and Karen.

"Would you like me to read it?"

Caroline nodded.

Iron Woman dried her hands. "Elizabeth's almost
finished. How about putting away the rest of the groceries?" She put on her glasses and leaned against the
sink.

Elizabeth counted six sheets of paper with writing
on both sides. Caroline was watching, too. When her
grandmother reached the last page, she stood still.
Iron Woman slowly refolded the papers and nodded.
Tears sprang into Caroline's eyes and her grandmother
opened her arms. They hugged, long and hard.

"Call the others to lunch, please," Iron Woman
whispered as she released her.

# Chapter
# Sixteen

Caroline never threw herself onto a chair the way Paul did, but Elizabeth noticed that she sat down more carefully than usual. She was fairly talkative, however, and lunch was much more cheerful than breakfast had been. The sandwich plate was empty before Sarah said, "Grandma, where's Molly?"

*Someone finally asked.*

"Still working." Iron Woman passed the cookies to Andrew and mustered a smile. "The lawn fete's this afternoon. Anyone want to go?"

The table erupted in noise as the Sheridans vied to explain what they had done, and what they had won, in previous years. Elizabeth thought it sounded awful—crowded and noisy and silly—but staying home did not seem to be an option. She pressed her lips together.

*You've survived worse.*

When the throng gathered on the porch, Elizabeth observed that Caroline had resumed her place on the swing. A book lay nearby on the floor.

*She's grounded. She can't come.*

Paul pantomimed to Caroline. She smiled and mouthed, "Thanks."

*He just promised to bring her something.*

Iron Woman came out, spoke briefly to Caroline, and patted her shoulder. They clamored off the porch and strolled into town. Except for trips to the grocery store, Elizabeth had not been into South Wales since the Fourth of July. It looked different, smaller, in the bright afternoon sunlight. From the pavilion, the carnival appeared to spread about a block in every direction.

Iron Woman went to buy tickets. She had explained that they could be used to play games, to enter raffles, or to buy food. Elizabeth's buddy for the afternoon would —*thank goodness*— be Petey.

"Hey, Andrew." Adam gave Elizabeth a narrow-eyed glance and pointed to a high-tech display. "Think they sell tracking devices?" His tone was light but tinged with sarcasm.

"Adam Joseph." The words were stone. "May I see you for a moment?"

Iron Woman marched half a dozen paces away

and remained with her back to the group. Adam set his lips in a thin line and followed her. They stood together briefly; then Iron Woman walked to a picnic table and waved the others toward her. After a minute, blushing and subdued, Adam joined them.

Iron Woman had purchased an entire roll of orange tickets. She spun a line of them across the width of the table, snapped it, and handed the result to an outstretched hand. Inside of a minute, each of them had been supplied with sixteen tickets. Elizabeth had planned to decline but was foiled when Iron Woman folded the last two strips together.

"Here are your tickets and Petey's. If he chooses a hot dog, please make sure he *sits down* to eat it." She put the remainder of the roll in her bag. "Have fun," she said to them both. Then she turned to Sarah. "What's first, partner?"

Sarah pulled her toward a miniature train ride. Elizabeth was left alone with Petey and a fist full of orange paper.

"What do *you* want to do, Turtle?"

Elizabeth shook her head. She had no idea. The crowd's noise left her dizzy, and Iron Woman's warning about hot dogs made her aware that Petey had been entrusted to her care. That terrified her.

"Let's *look* first," he said, taking her hand. His small fingers felt warm and damp and oddly reassuring.

They made their way between shoulders, past tables, and among booths. One could shoot squirt guns at candles, toss wooden hoops over bottles, or fish in a duck pond. One could throw baseballs galore: through holes, at bowling pins, and past machines that measured speed. There were dozens of raffles: for quilts, for a car, for pen and pencil sets, for scuba diving lessons. One could buy snow cones or pretzels or ice cream, and the smells of cotton candy and popcorn were everywhere.

Petey settled on the duck pond for his first activity. He won two plastic birds, a Chinese yo-yo, and a small metal truck. Satisfied, he handed his prizes to Elizabeth and asked to be taken to the car ride. Ten little vehicles rode in a circle, and each one made a noise. Petey chose the fire engine and rang the bell. As soon as it came to a stop, he ran to the end of the line and began to consider his next choice. He rode a sheriff car with a siren, a Model-T with a squeeze-bulb horn, the fire engine a second time, a racing car that sounded like a lawn mower, and a convertible whose noisemaker seemed to be broken. He grinned and waved each time he passed her.

"How many times so far?" Iron Woman came up beside her. There was laughter and sympathy in her voice.

"Six."

"Hi, Petey!" Sarah yelled and waved with both hands. "Grandma? Can we get some ice cream? Please?"

Iron Woman grinned. "You bet." She turned back

to Elizabeth. "Be sure to drink something. It's hot."
She smiled again and went off with Sarah.

Petey rode the fire engine one more time and then
announced that he was hungry. To Elizabeth's relief,
he chose cotton candy and grape juice. She added a
small cola to the order. It *was* hot.

They found a patch of shade and she watched him
explore the sticky pink fluff. He was normally a pretty
neat eater for a little boy barely four, but cotton candy
was tricky. In no time, it looked as though his hands
and face had been splashed with pink paint.

"Try some." He smiled. Elizabeth gingerly teased
off a small piece. It was horribly sweet and she was instantly thirsty. She took a sip of her drink and poked
a straw through the foil that covered Petey's juice. She
picked it up to offer it to him and put it back down.
He was sticking his hands together and, with considerable effort, pulling them apart. He did it several
more times; then he looked up at her with eyes that
clearly said, "Help!"

Elizabeth felt herself smile. "I'll get some napkins."

The thin white paper tore easily and shreds stuck
to the pink paste. She dipped a second napkin into her
drink and scrubbed. They grinned at each other as one
palm became visible. Ten minutes later, Elizabeth finished his hands. Armed with a new stack of napkins,
she tackled his face. The cold, wet paper tickled, and
he giggled and squirmed. Finally, she gave up and
handed him his drink. She carried the sticky napkins

to the trash and sat down again. The juice had turned Petey's tongue and lips purple.

They wandered among the raffles and guessing games. At each table, Petey asked her the same question: "What do you have to do here?" He decided to enter a drawing for a flower arrangement he thought his grandmother would like, and a contest in which the winner came closest to guessing how many pieces of candy were in an enormous glass jar.

"That'd be enough for everybody!" He looked up at her. "What number should we write, Turtle?"

Elizabeth considered. The candies were all the same size, but the bottle changed shape. It was about eight inches in diameter at the bottom and narrowed to three inches or so near the top. She counted the layers, made allowance for air space, and began to calculate. Petey watched her in mute fascination.

"Four hundred and eighty."

Petey's eyes grew wide. "How many for each of us? Don't count Grandma. She never eats candy."

"More than fifty. *If* you win."

He nodded happily and she helped him complete the entry.

Petey tried the train and the merry-go-round and decided he wanted to use the last of their tickets to ride the cars again. He rode three times before wistfully asking Elizabeth to check her pockets. Was she *sure* all the tickets were gone?

"Petey! You won!" Paul and Abby ran toward them.

"Won what?"

"We don't know." Abby pointed behind her. "But they said, 'The winner is Petey Sheridan.'"

"On the loudspeaker," added Paul, clearly impressed.

The four of them made their way through the crowd. Abby and Paul asked questions until they had the answer: Petey had won a jar containing four hundred and ninety-three pieces of candy.

"You're *rich*, Petey!" Paul shouted. "Want me to carry it?"

Petey nodded and grinned and threw his arms around Elizabeth's legs. "Thanks, Turtle!" He released her and clapped as Paul picked up the jar.

"There's Grandma," Abby cried. "Grandma! Sarah! Look what Petey won!"

Paul tottered toward his grandmother.

"Heavens!" Iron Woman hurried forward and reached for the jar. "Let me take it, Paul. My arms are longer."

"She told me what number to write, and I won!" Petey hollered.

"Congratulations, Petey!" His grandmother smiled at him over the top of the jar. As they started to walk, she groaned. "Nice work, Elizabeth!"

*Is she mad?*

Iron Woman grinned as Petey bounced along announcing to the world that he'd won—he'd *won!*—and Elizabeth decided Iron Woman wasn't angry.

They found Adam and Andrew right away. Andrew was holding two small plastic surfboards, which he'd won at the ball toss. They congratulated Petey.

"Would you like me to take that?"

*A peace offering?*

"Thank you, Adam."

Iron Woman handed him the jar and said she had a few tickets left. Did anyone want to have his face painted? Sarah wanted a cat, Paul chose a spider, and Abby picked a rainbow. Petey declined, and Elizabeth wondered whether he thought he had been scrubbed enough for one day. Iron Woman suggested a swim. Her grandchildren chorused their thank yous, and they started for home.

Smiling, Caroline greeted them on the porch. Paul handed her a bag of cotton candy and she gave him a hug. She admired the day's winnings and shook Petey's hand. In response to a questioning look from her grandmother, she shook her head no.

"Adam, when everyone's ready, please go ahead. I'll be down in a few minutes."

The Sheridans dashed into the house. Elizabeth sat on the swing and looked at her watch. The first bathing suit appeared at 4:21; the last one burst onto the porch at 4:24. They'd tied their best time.

Being grounded apparently meant restriction to home *plus* the beach. As they walked, Caroline listened to the afternoon's adventures with affection and interest. When they reached the sand, she led the pack into the water. Elizabeth watched them for a moment and then began to climb.

Her rock shimmered, and it burned through her shorts. There were no clouds in the sky and there was almost no breeze. Small waves sputtered quietly onto the beach. The air was cooler than it had been in town, but for the first time, Elizabeth wished she dared to go into the water.

*Just my feet?*

She shook her head.

*It would swallow me whole.*

The ocean was blue now, truly blue, the color of Petey's eyes. She found him waist deep in water. Caroline was showing him how to scoop water onto his face. He tried twice before being jolted by a wave. Caroline picked him up quickly. He looked surprised but not unhappy. A moment later he nodded and she put him back down.

*Tweet!*

"Too far!" Abby and Sarah retreated toward the sand. Adam gave them thumbs-up and dove toward a ball. He surfaced, retrieved it, and tossed it to Paul.

"How's the view today?"

Elizabeth turned and nodded twice. Iron Woman waved and crossed the sand quickly.

Elizabeth glanced at her watch. "A few minutes" had been forty-six.

Iron Woman dropped her towel and her sunglasses and jogged toward the ocean. She slowed briefly as the waves reached her thighs and then dove. Again and again, she sliced through the water. When she began to swim, she raised her arms in precise triangles that reminded Elizabeth of the fins she had seen at the aquarium.

*Part dolphin or shark?*

Andrew hollered something to Caroline. She picked up the surfboards he'd won and ran toward the water. Elizabeth turned back to the ocean. The sun had shifted and a breeze had begun to blow. It was no longer the same blue.

*Tweet! Tweet! Tweet!* Iron Woman sounded the call to come out of the water. Laughing and dripping, her grandchildren came. No trace remained of Sarah's chocolate ice cream, nor of Petey's cotton candy. The face paint had vanished. Iron Woman's hair was damp and dark and curled softly. They all looked fresh and clean and sunburned and . . .

*What?*

Elizabeth didn't know, but she wished she were part of it.

# Chapter
# Seventeen

Despite the after-swim glow, and despite the afternoon's successes, dinner was a quiet affair. Everyone was aware of Molly's continued absence. There were bursts of energy and chatter during bests, but afterwards, conversation grew listless.

During dessert, Petey spoke. "I miss Molly."

"Me, too." Iron Woman's eyes flickered from face to face. "We all do."

Elizabeth wandered outside, chose a spot halfway between the house and the barn, and sat down. One at a time, she pulled brown-edged blades of grass out of the ground.

*She likes her family. I'm sure of it.*

Elizabeth didn't pretend to understand Molly—they were polar opposites. But right now, they had something in common: they were outsiders.

The Sheridans clearly wanted Molly back. For some reason, she wasn't willing to do or say whatever was necessary.

*Why?*

It was different for Elizabeth. She'd been imported, and she knew she'd be leaving. She wondered why Molly and Caroline had reacted so differently. Something wiggled at the back of her brain. At the beach, what had she wished she were part of? She never wanted to be part of anything. Why had that thought come into her mind? Did it have something to do with Molly? She plucked the leaves from a piece of clover. Why did every encounter with a Sheridan result in difficult questions?

The back door banged. New truck in hand, Petey crossed the lawn and sat down without seeming to notice he'd done so. He examined the wheels of the truck, smiled at Elizabeth, and began to push it through the grass.

"I like you, Turtle."

*Liking people is dangerous, kid.*

"You shouldn't." She pulled out another dozen blades of grass.

Petey suddenly got to his feet and walked away, leaving his truck on the ground. When Elizabeth looked up, he had turned to face her. His fists were clenched, his chin was trembling, and his eyes were brimming with tears.

"I can if I want to!" he hollered. Then he raced past the clotheslines and vanished.

Elizabeth sat motionless, her breath stuck in her chest.

*What on earth came over* him?

"Elizabeth!" Caroline was marching toward her. Andrew was with her, and their eyes glinted dangerously. "What did you do to Petey?"

Her eyes widened.

*I didn't do anything!*

"He's *crying!*" Caroline pointed in the direction Petey had run. "He won't tell us what's wrong, but I know he was out here with you."

"Petey doesn't cry for no reason!" Andrew half shouted at her.

"All I said was . . ."

"What?" they demanded in unison.

Elizabeth shook her head. He *couldn't* be *that* upset because she'd said he shouldn't like her.

"Whatever it was, you had better come and apologize," Caroline said. "Right *now.*"

*The path of least resistance: do as you're told.*

They marched her to the porch and up the steps. Petey was in his grandmother's arms on the swing. His sobs slashed the dusk's stillness.

*This isn't real!*

But it was clear she'd better say something.

"Petey? I'm sorry."

He threw himself from his grandmother's lap. Shoulders hunched, eyes streaming, he faced her. "No you're *not!*" he screeched. "You *meaned* it." Chin thrust forward, he dared her to say that she hadn't.

*I did mean it. And I can't lie to him.*

Elizabeth nodded. "But I'm really sorry it hurt your feelings."

"I HATE you!" He darted past her. The screen door banged and his tiny feet pounded the stairs. Silently, quickly, Iron Woman followed him.

Confounded, Elizabeth stared at the swing.

*Apologizing made things worse!*

Abby had come onto the porch and was huddled near the steps with Caroline and Andrew. The three of them stared at her. Elizabeth walked to the door, pulled it open, and deliberately shut it behind her. Soundlessly, she climbed the stairs. In the corner between her bed and the window, she hugged her knees and waited for her brain to stop vibrating.

"Elizabeth."

Heart racing, she jumped to her feet. Iron Woman had come into the room without knocking.

"Petey is hysterical." Her voice was low, but it trembled. "He will not, or cannot, explain why. I need to know exactly what happened out back, and I need to know now."

Elizabeth spoke to her pillow. "I was sitting on the grass. Petey came out and sat down next to me. He started playing with his truck. He said, 'I like you, Turtle.' I said, 'You shouldn't.' Then he got up and yelled, 'I can if I want to,' and ran away." She took a quick breath. "Then Caroline and Andrew came to get me."

Iron Woman studied her carefully. Then she turned and disappeared. Elizabeth crawled back into her corner. This time, she kept one eye on the open door.

Footsteps. Whispers. Questions. The family had assembled outside the bathroom. Near the back stairs, a door opened and closed. The hall grew still.

"Petey's asleep." Iron Woman spoke softly. "But he was very upset, and I want him to stay in my bed tonight."

"What did she do to him?" Adam's voice was taut with anger.

"What happened wasn't entirely Elizabeth's fault."

"Then whose *was* it?" he snapped. There was a pause and then a mumbled "Sorry."

"Circumstances. We'll talk about it tomorrow. Adam and Caroline, please check the downstairs. I want to be in my room in case Petey wakes up. Good night, everyone."

Feet shuffled and voices murmured. Elizabeth

reached her bed in two noiseless steps, ducked under the blanket, and pulled it over her head.

A drawer slammed.

"Quiet, Sarah!" Abby whispered harshly. "Grandma'll kill us if we wake her up."

Flat gray light filtered through Elizabeth's bedspread.

"Why'd she say, 'Let her sleep'?"

"I don't know. I don't know *anything* around here anymore," Abby said crossly. "C'mon. Let's change in the bathroom."

The door closed. Elizabeth pushed back the bedspread and looked at her clock. She'd been awake for more than four hours. From 5:03 on, she'd sat by the window, watching the trees become matte silhouettes against a somber sky. At 7:20 Sarah had stirred. Elizabeth had quickly gone back to bed and Sarah and Abby had gone downstairs without her. She had returned to the window and had overheard an argument between Adam and Andrew.

". . . and Grandma's letting her get away with it!"

"You think *I* don't care about Petey? She tried to apologize, Adam. I heard her. You weren't even there."

"It's not just last night, Andrew. It's the whole summer. How come Elizabeth is the only one who doesn't have to follow the rules? Who doesn't get spanked? Who doesn't have to tell best? Who doesn't have to act like a human being?"

"She's *new!* She's not used to us yet."

"Oh, give it up, Andrew. How much getting used to does it take? She doesn't even *try*, and the rest of us have to put up with it. Tell me Grandma's being fair about that!"

"Pretty soon Grandma will treat her the same."

"Bull! I'll bet you five bucks that doesn't happen before we leave."

"Deal!"

"You'd better have the money," Adam snapped.

"*You'd* better! You're so open-minded, I'd bet you'd make a *perfect* adjustment to a brand-new family."

"Don't tempt me."

"*Boys!* That's enough!"

They fell silent at once. As she crawled back into bed, Elizabeth wondered how much of the argument Iron Woman had heard. She brooded and dozed until Abby and Sarah collected their bathing suits.

*I hope Petey's O.K.*

The thought was unwished for, but there it was, in front of her.

*Why did "You shouldn't" upset him so much?*

She tried to picture him covered in cotton candy but could only see him screaming at her. Yesterday's clothes felt twisted and tight. The tribe mumbled on the porch. The door banged and the sounds faded.

The urge to go to the bathroom came over her. After struggling for several minutes, Elizabeth decided that she couldn't wait. The door to Caroline and

Molly's room was still closed. Iron Woman's door was open. Her room looked the way it always did: spare and neat.

Her stomach rumbled as she brushed her teeth. She drank two glasses of water and tiptoed back down the hall. Yellow gray light from an overcast sky filtered around the window shades. All three beds were in disarray, testimony to three restless nights' sleep. Clothes were scattered, dresser tops were in chaos, and books had escaped from their boxes. The room looked disgruntled.

Elizabeth did not want to go to the beach and she did not want to go downstairs. This was it. She changed her clothes and began to put things to rights. She was tucking in Sarah's bedspread when there was a knock at the door.

*Too late to hide.*

She continued what she was doing. The door opened.

"I'm glad you're awake. We need to talk."

Elizabeth began to straighten Abby's covers.

*"Sit-down* talk." Iron Woman perched herself next to Elizabeth's pillow and pointed to the end of the bed. Elizabeth released her grip on Abby's blanket and sat down.

"Is Petey O.K.?" She spoke without meaning to.

"No." Iron Woman gave her a very intense gray look before shifting her gaze to Abby and Sarah's dresser. "He's not. He's better than he was last night, but he's a very long way from O.K."

Elizabeth bit her lip.

"Petey's very young still. He hasn't spent much time away from the family. His understanding of how things work is based on his experiences with us. Until yesterday, he thought the world was a pretty safe place."

Iron Woman put her elbows on her knees, leaned forward, and addressed the floor. "First Molly disappeared, then you rejected him. It was more than he could begin to understand."

"I didn't mean to hurt his feelings."

"I don't think you intended to, but you need to look at things through his eyes." She twisted her wedding ring and spoke very softly. "Imagine you're four years old. There's someone you enjoy and look up to. You spend a wonderful afternoon together. She takes you where you want to go, she helps you win a big prize. You make a special trip outside to tell her you like her, and she says you *shouldn't*."

She looked at Elizabeth. "If you shouldn't like *her*, then it makes sense that she doesn't like *you*."

*That's not what I meant!*

Iron Woman glanced at her watch. "I set the timer and told Petey I'd take him to the beach when it rings." She stood up. "Will you come with us?"

*Offer, or order?*

Elizabeth sat perfectly still.

"At least may I tell him you'll talk to him later?"

*Tell him anything. Just go away now.*

Elizabeth nodded. When the door banged, she watched Petey walk down the driveway holding his grandmother's hand.

# Chapter Eighteen

Almost two hours passed before she heard Sheridan noise. The tribe was headed for the clotheslines. Iron Woman and Adam were standing by the fence. Their voices were too low to hear, but there was no doubt that an argument was under way. Iron Woman put a hand on Adam's shoulder; he twisted away and angrily pointed at the house. She spread her hands; he folded his arms. Iron Woman spoke rapidly for a minute. Adam threw down his towel and walked into the street.

"Adam!"

He turned right. He didn't slow down; he didn't turn around. He was gone. Iron Woman snatched up the towel and marched into the house.

Elizabeth went to find Petey. As she had hoped, he

was playing near the back door. His shoulders curled away from her when she squatted down.

"I know you don't want me, and I'll go away in a minute. I just want to tell you two things. I'm sorry about last night," she said slowly, "And I *do* like you."

He kept his eyes on his car. "Grandma said so." His voice was flat. "But I didn't believe her."

"It's true. I do." Elizabeth swallowed hard. "A whole lot."

He glanced at her. She nodded, stood up, and walked back to the house.

"Adam has gone for a walk," Iron Woman said briskly. "Sarah, would you please pass the salt?"

*A walk is one way to put it. And, strictly speaking, it's true.*

Lunch was consumed with lackluster dispatch. The sharing of "Petey's treasure" for dessert brightened the group's spirits only slightly.

"I'm going to ask all of you to do different jobs this afternoon, so don't disappear from the table just yet. Elizabeth, would you please help me clear?"

*Why?!*

It was Paul's turn, and everyone knew it. "What have you done *now*?" hung in the air. Elizabeth's face burned as she walked to the kitchen.

"Molly's not making much progress on her own." Iron Woman spoke quietly and rapidly. "I'm going to ask the others to talk to her. I don't know how she'll react, and Petey's too vulnerable to risk having him here. I'd like you to take him into town."

Elizabeth blanched.

Iron Woman appeared not to notice. She took a piece of paper from the counter and a bill from her wallet. "Here's a list of things we need at the drugstore. He can look around and buy something small. On the way home you can take him for ice cream," she said evenly. "Can you handle all of that?"

Elizabeth met her gaze and nodded, and they went back to the dining room.

"Petey, your job is with Elizabeth. She knows what to do." Iron Woman kissed him gently. "Elizabeth, take a backpack. The peroxide will be heavy."

They didn't talk at all on the way into town. Petey walked stiffly, with unfocused eyes. Elizabeth wondered what he was thinking, but she wouldn't have dreamed of asking. Not only did a person have the right to keep his thoughts private, she was afraid of what Petey's might be. She was glad she had spoken to him before lunch. She was uncomfortable enough as it was.

The transformation that had taken place in South Wales was astounding. Not a trace remained of the fete: not a ride, not a booth, not a napkin on the ground. Where had Petey eaten his cotton candy? Elizabeth couldn't tell.

Inside the drugstore, she explained that he could buy something. He nodded but offered no display of enthusiasm. They found the toy aisle and Petey began his survey. Elizabeth perched herself on a half-empty bottom shelf and watched him.

He had stuffed his hands into his pockets, which was unusual. He examined each toy in a vertical row, took one careful step to the right, and repeated the process. He didn't smile or speak or touch anything. He looked very small in red sneakers, royal blue shorts, and an enormous gray shirt that Paul had out-grown. His arms and legs were tan, but his face was pale.

*He is very young.*

Petey returned to the fourth row and pulled some-thing down. "This," he said, handing it to her. It was a blue plastic tube of some sort. Elizabeth wanted to ask him what it was, but decided against it.

"We'll do the list and then pay for everything. We'd better get a basket."

He followed her as she collected toothpaste and hydrogen peroxide and half a dozen other small things. Outside, Elizabeth transferred their purchases from the paper bag to the backpack and offered Petey his tube. He shook his head.

"What kind of ice cream would you like?"

"Peach."

*Of course.*

Petey didn't start to eat until they had settled them-selves on a bench in the shade of a tree. Methodically, he turned and licked until the ice cream was flush with the cone.

"Do you remember your mom?" he asked without looking at her.

*Huh?*

"Not Aunt Karen. The mom that borned you."

*Why on earth is he asking me that?*

"What she . . . looked like?"

He shook his head. "No. *Her.*"

*He means who she was, on the inside.*

She hesitated. "Not really."

"Do you ever think about her?"

"Sometimes," she said slowly.

"When?"

*He's getting at something, but I don't know what.*

"Mostly when I look at my parents' picture."

He licked a pale yellow drip from his hand. "Do you miss them?"

*The way you miss Molly? Or some other way?*

"No. They died a long time ago."

"How old were you?"

"Five."

He finally glanced at her. Then he pushed himself off the bench and put the remains of the cone into a trash basket. "Can I have my looker now?"

*Your what? Oh, that blue thing we bought.*

He held it up to his eye and twisted it back and forth. "It's for seeing *differently.*" He thrust it at her.

Elizabeth peered through it. Some sort of lens broke the image into dozens of prismlike bits that sparkled when the tube was turned. She nodded and tucked it into the backpack. She shouldered the bag and they began the walk home. Halfway there, he stopped and turned toward her.

"Carry me?"

Elizabeth realized with alarm that he was exhausted. Somehow, she managed to get him off the ground. He put his arms around her neck, his legs around her waist, and his head on her shoulder. Awkwardly, she started forward. A block later, he was asleep. By the time Elizabeth turned into the driveway, her arms ached to the point where they trembled.

Iron Woman was sitting on the swing. When she spied them, she flew down the steps and over the grass.

"Is he all right?" With quaking tenderness, she took him from Elizabeth's arms.

"He asked me to carry him. Then he fell asleep."

Elizabeth watched terror fade from his grandmother's eyes.

"Thank you."

They climbed the steps to the porch.

"You must be tired. Why don't you put those things in the kitchen and get yourself something to drink?"

Elizabeth emptied the backpack onto the counter, placed the change and receipts next to the pile, and carried the backpack to the front hall. The swing creaked and she glanced through the window. Iron

Woman gently rocked back and forth, Petey sound asleep in her arms.

She tiptoed up the stairs. The door to Molly's room was still closed.

Abby and Sarah were changing. From their conversation it was apparent that Adam had not returned, that Molly still refused to speak, and that Petey was awake. They were leaving for the beach in five minutes.

Iron Woman sighed impatiently and reached for the sponge. It was the third time in as many minutes that she had spilled something. When she wiped the counter, she noticed the blinking light on the answering machine.

"It's Adam. Someone tell Grandma I'm spending the night at Brian's."

Iron Woman leaned on the stove. "Your timing is simply terrific, Adam," she said in a weary voice. "Brian who? Brian where?" she asked the machine crossly.

"Maybe Caroline knows."

Iron Woman spun around and looked at Elizabeth as though she'd never seen her before.

"Maybe she could call him. He could leave a message for Petey."

Iron Woman contemplated the floor. Then she nodded. "Please ask her to come down."

Caroline knew which Brian. After a quick look

through the thin South Wales directory, she reached Adam. He called back and left a reassuring message for his roommate. While Petey listened to the tape, Caroline and Elizabeth began to set the table.

"That was a good idea, Elizabeth. Especially since dinner ought to be a real barrel of laughs with *two* people missing."

"What if we ate outside?"

Caroline slowly put down the forks. "That really might help." She smiled. "I'll ask."

The answer was yes, and Iron Woman adjusted the menu to include corn on the cob. That always worked better outside. Dessert was watermelon, and they had a rousing seed-spitting contest, which Paul won when he hit the porch steps from ten feet away.

Iron Woman looked around at buttery chins and juice-covered elbows. The dishes could wait. How about an after-dinner swim? They could even change outside, by the clotheslines. Boys first, then girls. The idea was received with enthusiasm and much giggling at the thought of being naked out of doors, even for a moment.

When they returned, Petey replayed Adam's message. Andrew offered to let him sleep in his bed and promised him another installment of his Petey-is-the-hero epic. Elizabeth was relieved to see Petey give his brother a small smile.

It was Adam's night to do dishes. Thinking she

would have the kitchen to herself, Elizabeth volunteered. She was more than a little taken aback when Iron Woman sat down at the table and began to write something. She did not speak, and as far as Elizabeth knew, Iron Woman did not look at her. Nevertheless, it made her skin itch to have Iron Woman behind her. The situation was made worse by the fact that the food had hardened: it took longer than usual to get the plates clean. She loaded the silverware into the dishwasher and began to scour the pot in which the corn had been cooked.

"Thank you for doing the dishes, Elizabeth." Iron Woman taped something to the little refrigerator and went through the door to the dining room.

Elizabeth dried the pan and looked around the kitchen. The envelope on the fridge read *Adam.* Whatever Iron Woman had written, she had left it where he'd be certain to find it.

Alone in her room, Elizabeth put on her pajamas and arranged herself under the covers. When Iron Woman came to kiss Sarah and Abby, Elizabeth decided to stay where she was.

"Good night, Elizabeth." Iron Woman turned off the light.

*How does she know I'm awake?*

She pushed the question out of her mind. Sleep would have come quickly if Sarah and Abby hadn't begun to whisper.

"Abby?"

"Yeah?"

"You know Molly today?"

"What about her?"

"She looked like Elizabeth."

"I know." There was a pause. "I was scared, too."

A window shade rattled.

"Do you think Petey's O.K.?"

"I think so."

"Good night."

"Good night, Sair."

# Chapter
# Nineteen

Elizabeth was sitting on her rock, contentedly watching the water, when the ocean began to recede. It was as though someone had pulled the plug on a drain somewhere beyond the horizon. She watched, helplessly, as the water disappeared more and more quickly until nothing remained but damp sand.

*It's gone!*

She sat up. Her heart pounded and her chest ached. It took her several minutes to realize that she had been dreaming. Her pulse had slowed almost to normal when the telephone rang.

*Iron Woman must still be downstairs.*

She looked at the clock: 10:55.

*Or she's sleeping with her door open. I shouldn't be able to hear the phone.*

She heard a soft click and footsteps coming toward her.

". . . be long?"

*Caroline?*

A car door slammed softly. Elizabeth slipped out of bed and tiptoed to the window. The station wagon's taillights glowed red, winked once, and disappeared.

A cool, damp gust of air made her shiver. It had rained while she slept, and the smell of wet earth mingled with pine. Elizabeth pulled the blanket from her bed, wrapped herself in it, and resumed her watch by the window.

Twenty minutes later, the car turned into the driveway. Iron Woman and Adam crossed the lawn without speaking. She heard low voices in the front room and then slow steps outside her door.

*Caroline's going back to bed.*

Something creaked below the window, but the door hadn't slammed. Iron Woman was sitting on the railing, her back against the post. A glimmer of golden light spilled onto the porch from the front window, but it was too dark to see her face clearly. Except for one brief glance at the sky, Iron Woman sat very still.

"Grandma?" Iron Woman turned toward the sound. "Can we talk?"

"I was hoping you'd want to," she answered softly.

Adam sat down next to his grandmother. Something stuck out of the back pocket of his swimming trunks, a narrow white stripe in the dimness. He put his palms on the railing and straightened his arms so that his shoulders hunched up to his ears. He sat that way for several minutes. Finally, he spoke.

"It hurts to see everyone trying so hard and getting nothing back."

Iron Woman nodded. "Caring really stinks, doesn't it?"

They laughed together; then the night grew quiet again.

Adam shrugged. "I can't help feeling protective."

"It's one of your most endearing qualities, Adam." Iron Woman rubbed his back. When she let her hand fall, he turned to face her.

"I asked Abby why she pulled that stunt with the snake. She said she wanted to find out if Elizabeth was really a robot." He shook his head. "Hard to blame her, really. That girl never smiles, never talks, never does anything." He snorted. "Except sit on that rock."

Iron Woman sighed. "We're *all* struggling, Adam."

"Everyone except Elizabeth," he growled.

"*Including* Elizabeth."

Adam's sneakers thumped against the railing.

"Do you remember a night like this, when you were twelve? You and I were sitting on the swing, and you said you hoped our family would never, ever change."

"I remember," he said slowly. He sounded surprised.

"Petey wasn't born until the following June."

The silence returned and lasted three or four minutes.

"Elizabeth is not Petey," Adam muttered.

"Of course she isn't. But she has things to teach us, too."

"Like what?"

"Like not taking our family for granted. Like there are other ways of looking at things."

Adam shifted restlessly.

"Elizabeth isn't to blame for everything that goes wrong around here. The situation with Molly was half the reason Petey got so upset."

A damp breeze filled Elizabeth's nostrils with the smells of rain and rusting metal and she was suddenly afraid she was going to sneeze. She rubbed her nose hard and leaned forward again.

"Molly doesn't know how to get back on track, does she?"

"No, she doesn't," Iron Woman said sadly. "And we can't help her. Not until she admits that what she did was dangerous. And that she's responsible for the choices she makes."

She leaned forward and looked down. "I'm really worried about her, Adam." Her shoulders rose and fell. "She wasn't scared by how easily things got out of control. She isn't scared about what *could* have happened. And she certainly isn't trying to figure out how to do things differently another time."

"Should I try talking to her again?"

"I'd be grateful if you would. Time away from the family hasn't helped."

"I'll tell her what happened at Brian's tonight." He paused. "If that doesn't work, I'll resort to fraternal devotion." Adam folded his arms. "Cleverly disguised as a death threat."

"Sounds good to me." There was the barest hint of laughter in her voice.

A strong gust of wind blew the window shade inward, and Elizabeth ducked. It hovered above her head for a moment and then was sucked against the screen.

"I'm sorry about this morning." Elizabeth could barely hear Adam's voice.

"I know," Iron Woman murmured.

The quiet resumed.

"Sometimes . . ." Adam yawned and Iron Woman ruffled his hair.

"Time for bed. *One* of us had better be awake enough to lifeguard tomorrow." She looked at her watch. "Make that *today*."

With soft bumpings of feet and doors, they left the porch.

"Molly awake?" Adam mumbled through a mouthful of muffin.

"She's awake." Caroline's voice was tight.

"Still not talking?" he asked sympathetically.

Caroline shook her head and carried the basket of muffins into the dining room. Adam exchanged a quick glance with Iron Woman. As she picked up the orange juice, Elizabeth heard him take the back stairs two at a time.

Elizabeth was loading the dishwasher, Iron Woman was scrubbing the top of the stove, and, rather ineffectively, Sarah was sweeping the floor. When Adam came into the kitchen, Iron Woman paused and looked up.

He nodded. "I think so. She's writing you a letter." He gave his grandmother a very small smile. "She's still too ashamed of herself to *talk* to you."

"Thank you, Adam." Iron Woman closed her eyes for a moment. Then she resumed scrubbing.

Adam poured himself a glass of milk. "Haircuts first today?"

"Please. I haven't seen Paul's eyes in a week." Iron Woman wiped the stove and got out her wallet. "This should take care of the four of you, including tips."

"O.K." Adam swallowed the last of his milk and handed his glass to Elizabeth. She put it into the sink without looking at him.

"After, can we go swimming?" Sarah asked. Iron Woman nodded.

Adam smiled at Sarah. "Shouldn't be more than an hour."

He gave his grandmother a kiss and went out

through the dining room. As she rinsed Adam's glass, Elizabeth heard him bellow to the boys to hurry up with their chores.

She wandered onto the porch replaying the scene in the kitchen: morning jobs, haircuts, swimming.

*They're all acting perfectly normal. As though nothing ever happened.*

At breakfast, Iron Woman had simply said, "Adam is back, and he's upstairs talking to Molly." No one had asked questions, no one had commented—no one had even looked surprised.

*How can they do that?*

Elizabeth suddenly realized that she was standing where Iron Woman and Adam had spoken. Quickly, she crossed the lawn to the big pine. She sat down and idly began to make patterns with the dry needles.

"Hey, Elizabeth!" Andrew called. "You coming?"

Minus Iron Woman and Molly, the swimsuited tribe was making its way down the driveway. Pale lines framed the boys' faces.

*How long have I been sitting here?*

She scrambled to her feet. Breakfast had been later than usual, and there had been haircuts. The sun was already yellow and hot, and the damp breeze felt soothing.

Atop her beach lookout, Elizabeth sought to free herself of Sheridan thoughts. They crept unbidden back into her mind.

*They're all acting perfectly normal.*

The older boys were trying to do handstands between waves. There were shouts of encouragement and loud peals of laughter as they were knocked down again and again. Abby and Sarah were happily splashing each other, and Paul was putting the finishing touches on a young mountain. Caroline and Petey sat propped on their hands, letting the waves run over and around them. Petey spoke very briefly, and Caroline leaned over to kiss the top of his head.

"Ahoy, Elizabeth!" Iron Woman waved. Molly was with her.

Elizabeth lifted one hand. Then she watched them walk toward the water. Iron Woman said something. Molly nodded and called to Petey. Arms raised, he raced toward her. Molly scooped him up and hugged him hard. She put him down, kissed his forehead, and spoke for a moment. He smiled and went to give his grandmother a hug.

Caroline put an arm around Molly's shoulders. Heads close together, they waded into the waves. Caroline released her hold, said something with an evil grin, and dove. Molly shouted and plunged after her. They chased each other up and down the shore.

*How . . . ?*

Abby and Sarah were throwing water into the air, the boys had joined Molly's chase, and Iron Woman smiled as Petey dripped sand onto her feet.

*As though nothing had ever happened at all.*

# Chapter
# Twenty

The breakfast chatter was a wall of noise. Elizabeth listened long enough to be certain they were going to the beach and then retreated into her private thoughts.

*Eight days left.*

Only eight, but a pretty certain eight. She didn't think Kevin and Karen would do anything drastic in Iron Woman's house, in front of the family. They'd wait until they got home.

*Should I take the shells I found on the beach?*

Four of them were special. She had her sand dollar, of course, but that was different. It was in a plastic box, and it might have come from anywhere. But she knew exactly where she'd found these four. If the kids at the next place were nosy, they'd find them, and then they'd ask questions. She'd refuse to answer, but what if they took them? What if they broke them? No, having them in her mind was better. She'd take the shells back to the beach, or she'd give them to Petey. It didn't matter.

Someone asked her a question in an insistent voice.

"It doesn't matter," she repeated.

Silence fell and commanded her attention in a way that noise never did. People glared at her with cold eyes or stared down at their plates. Adam was looking at Iron Woman with triumphant defiance. Elizabeth wondered what made him risk it.

*Did I say something?*

"You may be excused when you finish." Although her plate was half full, Iron Woman carried it to the kitchen. Six people went with her.

Narrowed eyes cast down, Adam mechanically stuffed French toast into his mouth until his plate was empty. "Come on, Petey."

Petey had been looking at her with sad, searching eyes. Now he slid off his chair and soundlessly followed Adam.

*What on earth just happened?*

Low voices rumbled in the kitchen. Elizabeth decided she wasn't hungry and climbed the stairs. It was her turn to do the bathroom. She was anxious to get to the beach, so she applied herself to the task with energy. She looked around, satisfied. Then she noticed the quiet.

*Silence? At the Sheridans'?*

The tribe had already reached the end of the driveway. They usually called her when they were ready to go. Maybe they had, and she hadn't heard them. A block behind them, she walked to the beach by herself.

As she climbed her rock, her dream returned with troublesome clarity. The ocean was there, of course. The waves chided her: *always here, always here, always here.*

"Hey, look! A seagull!"

An unfamiliar voice. A sharp pain in her back.

"You mean a *spazz* gull." Two more sharp pains.

Elizabeth had been sitting tailor fashion and it was difficult to move quickly. She looked over her shoulder as her fingers scrambled for a hold on the rock. Something hit her cheek, just below her right eye. Her heart raced as she turned back toward the ocean and fought her way onto all fours.

*Who? Why?!!*

Her perch was small, and there was almost no room to maneuver. Crouching on her hands and the balls of her feet, she inched around to look at her assailants. Another stone hit her shoulder.

*Two boys. About Paul's age . . .*

One with black hair, one with red. Hands clenched, pockets bulging.

*Escape!*

Frantically, she looked around. There was an eight-foot drop on the far side of her rock. The only other way down lay over the boulders, directly toward her tormentors. Two large stones found their marks, one on her arm, one on her leg. She was cornered.

"Leave her alone!" The words boomed and echoed.

Elizabeth's eyes darted to the left. Adam was striding toward the rock, face set and eyes hard. The others surged up behind him. He stopped a dozen feet away from the rock throwers and put his hands on his hips. The tribe fanned out. Legs apart and arms folded, the older Sheridan kids stood on either side of him. Eyes wide and mouths pinched, Sarah and Petey stood like statues next to Caroline.

"Get out of here." Adam's voice was flat. "Now!"

The two boys backed up several paces. Then they turned and ran. Still balanced on fingers and toes, Elizabeth trembled.

"Are you all right?" Adam demanded.

She managed to nod.

"Do you want to go home?"

She nodded again.

"I'll take her." Caroline stepped toward the rock.

"You'd better tell Grandma what happened. *She* won't."

The tribe broke formation and milled around quietly.

"Elizabeth?" Caroline squinted up at her.

Feet first, she made her way down the rocks. When she reached the sand, Caroline pointed to her cheek. "You're bleeding," she said with alarm. "Come on."

Dazed, Elizabeth allowed Caroline to lead her up the beach, up the road, up the driveway, and up the stairs to the porch.

"Here. Sit down." Caroline eased her onto the swing. "I'll get Grandma."

*Why did they throw rocks at me?*

The door banged. Iron Woman's eyes widened and then narrowed when she saw the cut on Elizabeth's face. The door banged again and Caroline crossed the porch with a bowl of ice cubes and a towel.

"Thank you."

*What if Adam and the others hadn't come?*

Iron Woman knelt down and picked up an ice cube with the corner of the towel. Very gently, she rubbed it back and forth under Elizabeth's eye.

*Why?*

*What if . . . ?*

Iron Woman shook her head and turned her attention to a bruise on Elizabeth's arm. Caroline watched them. Her grandmother looked up.

"Thank you for bringing her home." She took another piece of ice from the bowl and held it against an angry welt on Elizabeth's leg. "Between questions and water, Adam must have his hands full. Do you want to go back to the beach?"

"O.K.," Caroline answered, but remained where

she was. At last she said, "I'm sorry they hurt you, Elizabeth," and went down the steps.

*She sounded exactly like Karen . . .*

For twenty minutes Iron Woman iced Elizabeth's bruises in silence. Twice, she returned to the cut on her cheek. When she raised Elizabeth's shirt to look at her back, Elizabeth heard her draw her breath through her teeth. When she finished, she gently patted her back with the towel.

"It's lucky you weren't alone." Her voice was quiet and sad. "There's no possible explanation for what those boys did, and I wish it hadn't happened." She paused, very briefly. "But let's be grateful the others were there."

*There had been another time . . .*

After school, when she'd lived at the Wilsons'. She'd been sitting on a cement wall at the edge of the playground, thinking about the ocean. Three boys had thrown stones at her. She'd run, and she'd gotten away. But no one had helped her, and certainly no one had iced her bruises.

*What is it about me that makes people throw stones?*

Both times, she'd been minding her own business. She'd never had friends, but she didn't bother people, either. And she'd never even seen these boys before.

"Would you like to lie down for a while?"

Elizabeth fought tears as she nodded.

*It will be safe inside.*

She offered no resistance as Iron Woman tucked her into bed.

*What if . . . ?*

She fell asleep wondering.

"I've packed you a sandwich and something to drink." Iron Woman's voice was low but firm. "Here are your sneakers. Five minutes."

Elizabeth walked with resentful and reluctant steps.

"I know you're angry with me," Iron Woman said. "Those boys frightened you and they hurt you. It happened, and we can't undo it." They walked another dozen paces. "But we are *not* going to let them ruin the rest of your summer by keeping you away from the beach."

They stepped onto the sand. Elizabeth looked up at her rock and tasted the terror she'd felt. Warily, she looked behind her. Then she followed Iron Woman to a familiar pile of sneakers and towels. She sat down, careful to keep her bare legs away from the burning sand.

"Here's lunch, when you're ready." Iron Woman placed a soft-sided bag next to her.

"Grandma, look!" Petey was holding something in both hands.

Taking shallow breaths, Elizabeth examined the beach. No redheads, no dark-haired kids the right size.

She turned toward the ocean. The breeze was strong and the waves were larger than usual.

*Do they look that way because I'm at eye level?*

They were definitely *louder*, whatever the reason. She listened closely. There were intriguing variations in the *swooshes* and *hisses*. These waves were more complex than the ones she'd heard from the rock. She began to match individual waves to their sounds and found that she got better at it with practice.

*Tweet! Tweet!* Iron Woman sounded the call for a head count. As the Sheridans came out of the water, Elizabeth pictured the way they had looked from the rock: unsmiling, determined, unmistakably a unit. No wonder those boys had run.

*They rescued me.*

She scanned the beach again. No threats were visible.

*Why did they help me?*

She wasn't one of them. They didn't like her. Had they felt sorry for her?

"Keep working on it, Elizabeth. It's important."

*Did I say something?*

Iron Woman was wearing her sunglasses. The rest of her face was blank, and there was no expression to read.

*Did I imagine she spoke?*

When she looked up, Iron Woman was waist deep in water and Petey was riding one hip. A wave splashed them and his happy chortle skipped across the sand.

*He's getting back to normal. I hope.*

Caroline and Sarah were playing catch with the ocean: tossing a ball into the waves, chasing after it as it washed onto the beach. Their laughter sounded far away, high pitched and bell-like. Abby was building something out of sand with a friend. Every few minutes they stood up to admire their work.

Molly and the boys were throwing a yellow plastic football back and forth. Elizabeth's mind wandered back to the question: why had they helped her?

"No *fair*, Adam!" Molly called.

That was it. The Sheridans had a strong sense of justice. It had been two-against-one, and she had been unarmed. They would have come to the defense of anyone in that position.

*Still, I should thank them.*

She decided she would do so at dinner.

Dessert forks clattered onto plates and feet shuffled impatiently under the table. Elizabeth slowly raised her hand.

"Elizabeth? Would you like to say something?"

She nodded and addressed her unused spoon. "To everyone. Thank you. For making those boys go away."

Iron Woman looked at her and then at Adam.

"You're welcome," he said, finally. "We're all sorry it happened."

Elizabeth didn't think about the morning again until she was putting on her pajamas.

"Ohhh!" Sarah cried. "Elizabeth! Your *back* . . ."

"It must *kill*," Abby explained sympathetically. "It's all purple and green."

When it was her turn to use the bathroom, Elizabeth pulled off her top and, twisting awkwardly, examined her back in the mirror. Three angry ovals looked back at her, two the size of a fist and one a bit larger. They *were* purple and green.

*They'd look worse, and they'd feel worse, if Iron Woman hadn't spent all that time rubbing them with ice.*

She went back to her room in a pensive frame of mind.

*"Thank you" only means "You did something nice."*

She found a piece of paper and a pencil. *Dear Mrs. Sheridan,* she wrote. *Thank you for putting ice where the rocks hit.* She signed it, folded it, and left it outside Iron Woman's door.

"I appreciated your note. How are you feeling?"

"Better."

"Good." Iron Woman flipped the first batch of pancakes and put the serving plate on the stove. "Would you pour the juice, please?"

They worked in silence for several minutes.

"Would you like to talk about yesterday?"

Elizabeth stiffened.

*It happened. It's over. What is there to talk about?*

She shook her head.

Iron Woman glanced at her, poured the next round of pancakes, and set three bananas and a knife on the table. "At breakfast, you said we don't matter."

*I don't remember saying that.*

"Later, for no reason at all, two strangers threw rocks at you." She turned the pancakes. "The 'don't-matters' made them stop."

Elizabeth began to slice the bananas.

"One don't-matter brought you home. Another one tended your wounds."

*I said I didn't want to talk about it.*

"Against your will, you were forced to return to the scene of the crime." She got out the butter. "After dinner, you managed to say thank you. Not once, but twice."

*I wish I hadn't!*

"That's rather a lot to have happened in one day," Iron Woman said slowly. "Talking might help you sort it out."

Soundlessly, Elizabeth bolted.

## Chapter
## Twenty-One

 Elizabeth found herself under a bush, out of breath, and holding a knife in her hand. She couldn't remember leaving the kitchen.

*Where am I?*

Through heart-shaped leaves she spied a silvery board.

*The barn. I'm somewhere behind it.*

A drop of water slid down her neck and she shivered. Her arms and legs were wet. So was her shirt. The ground was dry, but dew shimmered on the leaves around her.

"Elizabeth?"

*Iron Woman!*

Her heart galloped.

"I'm sorry. I didn't mean to upset you."

*Go away!*

"You can stay out here if you want to, but I need to know you're all right."

*I'm not.*

"Elizabeth?" A pause. "If I know that you're safe, I'll leave."

*It's a deal.*

"I'm safe!"

Silence.

"Thank you."

The relief in Iron Woman's voice was palpable. What else was there? Elizabeth couldn't tell.

"I'm going back to the house."

*. . . ninety-eight, ninety-nine, one hundred.*

Elizabeth crawled out from under the bush, getting wet again in the process. The sunshine felt reassuring. She stood still for a moment, letting it warm her.

*What made me run?*

She replayed the scene in the kitchen. Nothing Iron Woman had said was news to her.

*Wait. Something I didn't say.*

"At breakfast, you said we don't matter."

She hadn't said that.

*Breakfast. Shells.*

She had been thinking about her shells. She would put them back, or she would give them to Petey. She would decide later. It didn't matter.

*It doesn't matter.*

That's what she'd said. It doesn't matter.

Had someone asked her a question? Had they thought "It doesn't matter" was an *answer?*

She sat down and replayed it twice more. She was pretty sure someone had asked her something, but she had no idea *what.* She shook her head. She simply couldn't remember. She'd have to let go of it for now.

A warm breeze stirred the leaves overhead. Dew had soaked through the seat of her shorts. An ant tickled her as it crawled across her knee.

*Do you even know the ocean exists?*

The ant changed direction twice, crawled onto her sneaker, and vanished. She put her hands in her lap and realized she was still holding the knife. Listlessly, she stuck it into the ground. Restlessly, she pulled it out again.

*What day is this?*

It was Saturday. Petey's parents were coming tonight. So were Adam and Molly's. Kevin and Karen would be here tomorrow.

Elizabeth hadn't thought about them in a long time. She wondered if they would look different. Her mind floated back to the first time she'd seen them: Kevin's dark brown hair, discerning blue eyes, and Sheridan smile; Karen's auburn curtain of hair, dark-lashed green eyes, and gentle smile.

Kevin was a lot like his mother, she decided, but less intense. Like all the Sheridans, he looked directly at you, but not *through* you the way Iron Woman did.

Karen? She moved more slowly than the Sheridans and spoke more softly. Elizabeth appreciated both things.

*She's a hugger, though.*

It had taken Karen about a week to get the message that Elizabeth didn't like to be touched. Even then she forgot, and when Elizabeth flinched, she would apologize. She supposed it was difficult for Karen to remember: her children were huggers. They came by it naturally, got it from both sides of the family. Caroline and Paul were a cross between Kevin and Karen.

*Today's brilliant thought.*

Of course they were. Paul was a bit more like Kevin, Caroline a bit more like Karen. Maybe sixty percent and forty percent. But each kid clearly belonged to both parents.

Elizabeth wondered if she resembled *her* parents. It was becoming harder and harder to remember them without looking at the picture. Because they never aged or changed expression, they had gradually become less real, more like dolls. She wondered what things would have been like had they lived, and then impatiently dismissed the thought from her mind. They were dead. They had been dead for more than half her life. There was nothing to be gained by playing "What if?"

It was equally stupid to speculate about the next set of foster parents. They'd be what they'd be, and somehow she'd manage. All in all—except for refusing to leave her alone, and except for Iron Woman— the Sheridans had been the best.

The Wilsons had been gruesome, the Hartricks merely awful. They had considered adopting her but had decided against it. She'd learned the value of eavesdropping while she'd been there: when the social worker had come to collect her, she hadn't batted an eyelash.

The situations before that had all been temporary. The foster parents had known it; she had known it. This Sheridan thing was supposed to be an adoption placement, but when Kevin and Karen arrived, they would know what she knew. It would never work. She would never, ever fit in.

*I don't laugh. I don't talk if I can help it. I don't understand why people say and do things. I don't play. I don't swim. I don't hug.*

It was hopeless. They would see it was hopeless, and it would be over.

*At least I've seen the ocean.*

She wondered when they'd send her back. Probably before school began. She hoped so. She hated changing schools in the middle of the year. If you were new in September, no one really noticed. If you came in the middle, they always asked questions.

"Turtle?"

Elizabeth's eyes jerked toward the sound. Petey's forehead was puckered.

*He's not sure if I want him to be here.*

Deliberately, she nodded twice.

"Grandma said you need to be by yourself."

Elizabeth nodded again.

"No one's supposed to come back here." He paused. "Abby said I'll get spanked . . ."

*Then why . . . ?*

". . . but I thought you might need me."

*How odd!*

Elizabeth's eyebrows drew together. "I do."

The lines vanished from Petey's forehead. He took three more steps and sat down.

"Do you remember yesterday, at breakfast? When everybody stopped talking?"

Petey nodded eagerly.

"Did someone ask me a question?"

"Caroline."

"What did she say?"

"'Don't you care at all what the rest of us think?'"

*It doesn't matter . . .*

"I *knew* you weren't listening!" He bounced. "You didn't hear her, did you?"

She shook her head slowly. "I was thinking about something. Something else."

"What?"

Elizabeth looked into his earnest face. He wasn't being nosy; he was interested.

"Seashells."

He nodded. Somehow, Petey understood that it

was possible to think about seashells. That it was possible to think about them so hard you didn't hear the person next to you.

*It matters. I'll give them to you.*

"Are you finished being alone?"

Petey had helped her to understand one thing, but Elizabeth could feel bits and pieces of other questions poking her brain. Daring her, taunting her, *warning* her to sort them out.

"Not yet."

Petey's shoulders drooped, but he said, "O.K.," and stood up.

"Just a little while longer."

He started back toward the house and then suddenly stopped. "Can I tell Grandma? That you didn't hear Caroline?"

"Then she'll know you came out here."

"She probably knows already." He sighed. "She knows everything."

"You can tell her," she said slowly. "Tell her I said you helped."

Petey disappeared.

*Don't spank him. Please.*

Elizabeth really hoped that she wouldn't. He'd already been spanked because of her. She didn't want to think about it.

*It matters.*

Petey matters.

*So do the others.*

Elizabeth caught her breath. They *did*. She didn't *like* the fact that they mattered, but there it was.

*When did that happen?*

She considered each of them. Adam. Caroline. Molly. Andrew. Abby. Paul. Sarah. Petey. She would miss them.

*Damn it!*

The knife caught her eye and she began to flick little triangles of mud into the air. She had dug a sizable hole before her mind cleared.

*It's going to be hard enough to leave the ocean. I can't deal with leaving* people, *too.*

She would have to make them *un*matter.

Elizabeth knew she could do it. She'd done it before. There had been three: her second-grade teacher, the one who'd given her the sand dollar; the youngest Hartrick; and the librarian who'd given her the bookmark.

She sighed. It took a lot of energy to unmatter people. And there were so *many* of them! But it was better that she knew. She didn't want to imagine what might have happened if she'd been caught by surprise.

Would she have to unmatter them all? Even though Adam plainly loathed her, he had rescued her. The others looked up to him. He mattered.

She resigned herself to the effort and called a picture of Adam into her mind: a three-dimensional, technicolor picture. When it was clear, she held it there. Slowly, she began to flatten and fade the image.

It grew smaller as it lost its color. When it was the size of a postage stamp—a colorless, sterile, little snapshot—she stopped.

*One down, seven to go.*

She had trouble with Caroline and got stuck again on Paul, but she kept at it until they succumbed.

*One more.*

Petey looked at her with his searchlight eyes. He refused to shrink. He refused to fade. A little voice of panic said he wasn't going to.

*I'm tired. I'll rest for a minute, and then it will happen.*

She tried again. She tried until she had a raging headache.

*It's too bright out here. I'll do Petey tonight, when it's dark.*

She stood up before she remembered that she hadn't figured out what made her run from the kitchen. She'd deal with that later, too.

Iron Woman was hanging laundry. A few feet away, Petey was playing with a dump truck. He crossed the grass to meet her.

"Thank you for coming to find me before."

"You're welcome."

"Did you get spanked?"

He nodded. "Grandma means it when she says not to."

"I'm sorry anyway."

He gave her a small smile and, together, they walked to where Iron Woman was working.

"I'm glad you're back." She bent down to get another sheet from the basket. "When I'm finished, would the two of you like to go to the beach?"

They looked at each other and nodded.

"Then, Petey, go and get changed. Elizabeth, there's a sandwich for you on the counter."

# Chapter
# Twenty-Two

As Iron Woman's grand-children came out of the water, Elizabeth examined each of them carefully. It had worked. She could superimpose their unmat-tered images when it was necessary, and she followed them home feeling armored.

Steve and Elena, and Tim and Rachel, were scheduled to arrive within the hour. Everyone changed quickly and hovered near the front door. Elizabeth began to feel prickly and decided to watch from her window.

Tim and Rachel pulled into the driveway and their children leapt from the porch. Abby reached the car first, followed by Sarah. Hand in hand, Petey and Andrew raced after them. Elizabeth felt spiders crawl over her neck. Impatiently, she brushed them away and counted eight sets of hugs. Iron Woman crossed the lawn and brought the total to ten. Nieces and nephews tumbled after her.

Before the newcomers reached the house, a second car pulled in—Steve and Elena. Adam and Molly separated from the pack. They didn't run, but they walked very quickly. Elizabeth lost count of enthusiastic and haphazard embraces. The pricking sensation in her neck turned into a disagreeable burning and she stole her way out to the barn.

The pine trees were silent and static and safe.

Family dinner was a horror. Rachel passed Elizabeth her turn at best. She chose the potatoes and passed her turn to Caroline without realizing she'd already spoken. Awkwardly, Caroline repassed her turn to Steve.

Elizabeth went to bed wishing that tomorrow were over.

In a foul mood, she woke up thinking the same thing.

Kevin and Karen were supposed to arrive mid-afternoon. During lunch, Iron Woman reported that Kevin had called. They'd had car trouble but would be there before dinner. Elizabeth's skin crawled. She was exhausted from holding her breath. Exhausted enough to approach Iron Woman as the tribe gathered for the afternoon swim.

"May I stay here?"

Iron Woman looked at her for a long time before she answered.

"No."

That was it. No questions, no reasons, nothing but no. Elizabeth nursed her anger all the way to the beach. She sat as far away from the towels as she dared and scowled at the sand. Every few minutes, Iron Woman's eyes flickered in her direction.

*Have you considered a ball and chain?*

She hugged her knees and wished that something would happen to keep Kevin and Karen from arriving or, better yet, that something would make Elizabeth Lawson disappear into thin air.

Two hours and six minutes later, Iron Woman said something to Steve and left the beach. At five o'clock, he blew his whistle. Elizabeth walked to the house half a block behind the last Sheridan. Steve looked back three times and waited at the foot of the driveway until she passed him.

*Or a leash?*

She climbed the stairs and stood to one side of the window. The others gathered on the porch and the lawn. The car pulled in. Before the engine stopped running, she had locked herself in the bathroom.

Eight minutes passed before there was a knock at the door.

*Not Iron Woman. Please!*

"Elizabeth?" It was Caroline.

"What?"

"Mom and Dad are here!"

*No kidding.*

"Coming."

When the second hand of her watch had completed two circles, Elizabeth flushed the toilet and washed her hands. As she opened the door, she heard Kevin's resonant laugh. A moment later, Karen's voice floated up the front stairs. Elizabeth's jaw tightened as she walked toward the sound. When she reached the landing, Karen turned around and smiled up at her.

*No!*

Elizabeth felt as though she'd been punched in the stomach. Her fingernails dug into her palms. She squeezed her eyes shut and felt her tongue push against her teeth.

*Damn it! Damn it! Damn it!*

It was worse than she'd feared. *Much* worse. But she would have to deal with it later. She couldn't stand where she was any longer. Bending her knees with difficulty, she forced herself down the remaining steps.

Karen put her hands lightly on Elizabeth's shoulders. "Hello, Elizabeth."

She flinched as though she'd been burned and Karen let her hands fall.

"Hi." She could barely hear herself over the pounding in her ears.

"How *are* you?" Kevin asked.

Elizabeth flinched again. Her nervous system reacted to Kevin's voice the way it did to seeing Karen.

*Damn it!*

She struggled to breathe.

"Look! It's finished!" Paul bounced toward them, grinning and waving his math book. His parents smiled as he flipped through the pages. When he had shown them the whole book, Karen gave him a hug.

"Congratulations!" Kevin took two five-dollar bills from his wallet.

"Thanks, Dad!" Paul thrust one of the bills at Elizabeth and his parents looked at him with puzzled expressions. "She helped me," he explained.

Elizabeth drew in a quick breath and spoke to the floor. "No, thank you." She took a step backwards. "May I be excused?"

Without waiting for an answer, she went steadily up the stairs, quietly closed the door, and pressed herself into her corner.

*It isn't* fair!

Every cell in her body screamed in frustration. She didn't *want* to feel this way! She *hadn't* missed them. She *hadn't!* Waves of baffled anxiety coursed through her. She hadn't seen them in almost a month. Unmattering *them* never entered her mind!

The door opened and Caroline slammed a glass of ice water onto Elizabeth's dresser. "In case you'd like to *warm up* before you talk to Mom and Dad again."

*What?!*

"Thanks for giving them such a wonderful start to *their* vacation." Caroline closed the door hard.

*I didn't do anything!*

Elizabeth's stomach muscles tightened.

She hated Caroline.

And she hated Caroline's parents.


"Din-ner!" Molly's voice rang up the stairs.

*You can handle this, Lawson.*

She had unmattered the others, and she simply wouldn't look at Kevin or Karen. Or Petey. His image had refused to surrender last night, and now he came in for his share of her anger.

Elizabeth served herself, found a place near the kitchen door, and moved food from her plate to her mouth until it was Kevin's turn to tell best.

"Being here, with all of you," he said. "Even if it means putting up with Mom's cooking." The room burst into laughter.

"No dessert for you, Kevin!" his mother retorted, and they all laughed again.

When Kevin passed his turn to Andrew, Elizabeth mumbled, "Excuse me," and slipped into the kitchen. She flew up the back stairs and tiptoed the length of the hall. Her litany was of no use. Mental gymnastics *might* help. She squared all the numbers from one to twenty-five and then began to multiply two by itself. She reached 16,384 before she heard footsteps. Large, *male* footsteps.

Kevin stood just inside the doorway. "We're going for an after-dinner swim. Can you be ready in five minutes?"

Elizabeth shook her head.

"You can walk, or I can carry you, but you're coming," he said evenly. "Which one will it be?"

Kevin was perfectly capable of carrying fifty-seven pounds as far as the beach. Elizabeth stood up. Without looking at him, she walked around the end of the bed, past him, and down the stairs. She barreled across the lawn to the driveway. Then she slowed her pace. There was a clump of Sheridans ahead of her and she had no desire to overtake them.

She had no desire to listen to them, either, but the wind was blowing toward her. They were going to an amusement park tomorrow. Everyone, even Iron Woman. There were only six ocean days left, and now one of them was going to be squandered at some stupid park.

*Maybe they won't go if it rains.*

She looked up. Clouds overlapped each other: a muddy yellow gray, a cold purple gray, the white gray of dirty snow. The sun was not visible except as a horizon-bound patch of gray somewhat lighter than the rest. The road was gray. When they reached the sand, that looked gray, too. Against it all, Elizabeth's confusion and fury glowed neon orange. She watched with contempt as the first wave of Sheridans ran toward the water.

She heard voices behind her and shifted her stance so that her right shoulder faced the path. The rest of the family arrived at the same time. Her eyes became slits as she backed toward her rock. She was glad Iron Woman was with them. It made her anger burn brighter.

When the last Sheridan had splashed its way into the water, Elizabeth stormed around the end of her lookout and onto the rocky part of the shore.

The ocean seesawed in the flat light. At first soothing, its monotony became irritating. Laughter rang across the water. Abruptly, there appeared in front of Elizabeth a lineup of unmattered Sheridans. One by one, in rapid succession, they burst back into color. When the last one was whole, a vermilion explosion rocked her mind.

Her chest heaved and she shook. They *couldn't* be here! She took ragged breath after ragged breath, in total despair. She knew she would not be able to unmatter them a second time.

Magenta rage rose within her.

*I'll drown them instead.*

She threw Petey first. The stone disappeared without a splash and her fury increased. She grasped two more rocks and hurled Abby and Sarah. She cast

Andrew as far as she could. Uncaring, she pitched in his parents. Molly followed them quickly. Elizabeth flung Adam into the depths and then tossed in *his* parents. This rock would do for Paul, that one for Caroline. She heaved them into the air and felt her chest burn. In a frenzy, Elizabeth grabbed two more rocks and leaned back. Kevin first, then Karen. They disappeared within a foot of each other.

Now to dispose of Iron Woman, once and for all. Elizabeth picked up a flat, lopsided stone and walked as close to the water as she dared. With both hands, she heaved it past her hip. A wave washed over it and retreated, leaving a halo of speckled white foam.

*Take her!*

She couldn't move the stone without touching the water.

*Take her! Take her!*

A wave spun the rock sideways. Another surge yanked it a few inches farther and her frenzy began to subside. Three waves later, the stone vanished. Elizabeth watched the spot where it disappeared, defying it to come out of the water.

It did not.

They were gone.

*All* of them.

"Elizabeth?"

She whirled toward the sound. Kevin was standing a dozen feet to her right, poised to walk toward her. The sky had grown darker, and it was difficult to see his features. His mother stood behind him, a charcoal silhouette under the overhang of the rock that had once been Elizabeth's refuge.

She snapped her eyes back to the water.

*You let them escape!*

The waves rippled languidly. The ocean had betrayed her; now it mocked her. Why had she ever cared about it at all?

Elizabeth lifted her chin. She wouldn't even *bother* to hate it.

She walked past Kevin, made a detour around his mother, and began the trip back to the house. Some part of her was aware of being followed, but it didn't matter. As far as she was concerned, they could stand by the rock for the rest of their lives.

Sheridan noise sounded discordant and flat. As she marched up the steps, someone said something to her. She didn't know who, and she didn't care what. Without pausing, she went into the house and up to her room. In the dark, she pulled down the shade and pried off her sneakers. Beneath the blanket, she folded her arms, closed her eyes tightly, and walled off the world.

She was standing alone on the beach. Once again, the ocean began to recede. The water disappeared with irritating slowness. It *knew* it had to go. Why was it taking so long? At last, the ocean was empty. It was gone, and no one would miss it.

The horizon shifted. Darkness rose into the sky as the wall of water grew taller. It began to move. There was no place to run. There was nothing to do but watch as the tidal wave sped toward her. It towered over her, blocking the sky and the light. It began to fall.

When she woke up, she knew she was dead.

# Chapter
# Twenty-Three

The trip to the amusement park would take 270,000 seconds.

Elizabeth sat on the lawn, next to the car, wishing she hadn't figured that out. Wishing she had never come to South Wales. Wishing she had never met Kevin and Karen Sheridan.

The throng began to bang its way onto the porch and her head started to ache. She heard Kevin's voice and wished she were deaf. More people came onto the porch and the first bunch spilled onto the lawn. She stared at the grass and wished she'd never been born.

Karen's sneakers appeared in front of her. She hoped Elizabeth was feeling better this morning, and she was sorry she hadn't been able to eat breakfast. There was a drugstore near the amusement park.

Motion-sickness pills might allow her to enjoy some of the rides, and the trip home would be easier.

Spiders crawled over Elizabeth's back and down her arms.

"Elizabeth?" Karen squatted down.

She closed her eyes tightly.

"Please look at me."

*I can't!*

Her breath came in gasps.

"Please?" Karen ran a finger down her cheek.

Something exploded at the base of Elizabeth's neck. "I *won't!*" she shrieked. "You can't make me!" she panted. "I never want to see your *stupid* face again!"

Her ears rang. They clanged into silence and she opened her eyes. There were three pairs of sneakers in front of her. Kevin was standing on one side of Karen. Iron Woman stood on the other.

"Elizabeth, come down here."

Iron Woman's voice was cold. Elizabeth bit her lip. She wished those words—what had she said?—hadn't burst into her mind and out of her mouth. She wished she were sitting in the back seat of the car. She didn't want to be alone with Iron Woman. She didn't want to face those X-ray eyes.

"*Now.*"

As she forced her feet forward, her litany rolled through her mind. Mechanically, she walked down the stairs.

Iron Woman pulled a chair into the middle of the room. "Sit."

Elizabeth lowered herself onto the seat and glued her eyes to the leg of a table. She waited, tense and alert, for whatever was next.

Seconds turned into minutes. The silence tasted like chalk. She tried to concentrate on breathing with her mouth closed. She tried not to think about the fact that Iron Woman was looking at her. She traced the edge of a floorboard three times with her eyes.

*Say something! Do something!*

The quiet was excruciating. Some part of her realized that the tables had been turned: silence had always been *her* ally. People had grown frustrated or bored and had left her alone.

*That isn't going to happen this time.*

A tiny moth of panic flickered to life in her stomach. The stillness continued, and it fluttered its way into her chest.

"What do you want to be when you grow up?"

Elizabeth felt her brain bounce. It took several beats of her heart to recover and several more to make sense of the words.

*What . . . ?*

Where had that question come from? What did she mean? Elizabeth looked madly from one table leg to another.

*What's the right answer?*

"Have you given any thought to the future?"

A buzzing sound swept up the back of her neck and into her ears. She shook her head, trying to clear it. The sound only got louder.

"No." The word was a croak.

Elizabeth felt her eyes widen. She *hadn't* given it any thought. Beyond her dream of seeing the ocean, she never thought of the future. Today was always enough of a challenge.

"What about the next couple of years?"

The buzzing in her head sounded like flies against a window screen. She tried to swallow but couldn't. She had always been able to figure out what they wanted her to say. She'd done it with social workers and psychologists and foster parents. Why wouldn't her brain help her? She wished she could retreat somewhere to figure this out. Calmly, one step at a time. But Iron Woman was waiting.

"I don't know."

The buzzing became a high-pitched whine.

"Where will you be, on Christmas, when you're Caroline's age?" Iron Woman's words were distant and thin.

*Christmas? What is she talking about? What is she getting at?*

Elizabeth grasped at the numbers. Caroline was fifteen. Christmas was in December. Three years and five months from now. Where would she be? She didn't know. Last Christmas she'd been at the Wilsons', the one before that at the Hartricks'. The one before that? She shook her head. She couldn't remember. She didn't *want* to remember. Who *cared* about Christmas?

A picture forced its way into her mind. It was small and far away, but oddly bright. The picture grew larger. It was Christmas. The last one, the year she was five. The tree was a mass of twinkling lights and shiny red ornaments. Her parents sat next to it, wearing their bathrobes and smiling.

Elizabeth drew in a sharp breath and the picture vanished. She felt disoriented, as though she hadn't slept in a very long time. Slowly, she remembered where she was. Her eyes darted across the floor. Iron Woman hadn't moved.

*What was the question?*

"Do you want to spend that Christmas here?"

*Christmas with the Sheridans? Family dinner, a thousand times worse!*

"No!"

Her head pounded.

*Why won't she stop asking questions? Why is she doing this?*

Iron Woman crossed the room. "Then why did you agree to live with Kevin and Karen?"

Elizabeth couldn't think. She couldn't catch her breath.

"To see the ocean!"

The silence resumed. A breeze stirred and bits of dust swirled across the floor. A truck rumbled past the house. The slow, rhythmic ticking of the clock was a lifeline. Elizabeth began to count the seconds. She reached two hundred and eighty-six before Iron Woman moved.

*Maybe she's giving up.*

Elizabeth allowed herself a small glimmer of hope. From the corner of her eye she saw Iron Woman take something from Karen's tan canvas bag. It was dark blue and flat, the size of a postcard. She recrossed the room, stopped directly in front of Elizabeth, and held the little book toward her.

"Open it."

The stiff pages unfolded by themselves. It was a bankbook of some sort. There was only one entry, opposite a pale blue number one: Friday's date, $200.00 under the heading "Deposits," and the same amount under "Balance." The rest of the page was blank.

*What am I supposed to make of this?*

"Now look at the inside cover."

Elizabeth turned the page. Account number 27-1503391. Day-to-Day Deposit. Kevin T. Sheridan and/or Karen G. Sheridan. Below their names, Karen had written, *Elizabeth—college.*

The little book slid from her fingers.

They were saving money to send her to college?

They weren't planning to send her back?

They were going to *keep* her?

It wasn't possible.

It *wasn't.*

"Do you know what a 'commitment' is, Elizabeth?"

Iron Woman bent down to pick up the book.

"It's more than a responsibility. It's a pledge, a promise. Kevin and Karen made a *commitment* to be your parents. To care for you and protect you and teach you and love you. Forever."

The floor lurched. Elizabeth clutched the chair and frantically tried to hold back a scream.

"Look at me."

Unable to stop herself, Elizabeth did as she was told. Iron Woman's charcoal eyes shimmered.

"They *made* that commitment the day they brought you home. They have *kept* that commitment in every way they know how." Her chest heaved. "And in return, you have done every single thing that you could," she bit off the words, "to kick them in the teeth."

Elizabeth closed her eyes. Hot tears ran down her cheeks, and the scream in her chest turned into a sob.

"You've *hurt* them, Elizabeth. Kevin and Karen. And Caroline and Paul. You've hurt the whole family. We've *all* tried, again and again. You've pushed every one of us away." Her voice shook. "And what you said to Karen this morning was nothing short of *cruel!*"

The tears flowed harder.

It was true.

She had been *loathsome* to Karen.

Admitting that somehow allowed her to see things through Sheridan eyes. They had thought she had joined their family for good. Her attempts at self-preservation must have been seen as brutal rejection.

Elizabeth sobbed, no longer trying to stem the tears, no longer wanting to.

She cried because she had hurt Petey; she cried because Andrew had defended her; she cried because Abby and Sarah were afraid of her; she cried because she hadn't heard Caroline's question; she cried because Adam hated her; she cried because Kevin and Karen apparently didn't. She cried because she was the way she was and she didn't know any other way to be.

She cried for a long, long time. She lost all sense of where she was, or with whom. Something inside of her had come undone, something she could feel but not name. Finally, slowly, her tears spent themselves, and she became aware that she was being offered a tissue. She wiped her eyes and blew her nose.

"I'm glad to see you have a conscience."

Iron Woman moved another chair and sat down. Elizabeth desperately wanted to be by herself, but she hadn't the strength to stand up, much less to run. She took several slow breaths and heard the clock ticking again.

"It's a pity you have no sense."

Elizabeth took another tissue and tried to jump-start her brain.

*No sense?*

"*Every* kid deserves a family, Elizabeth. Even kids

who don't want one. Even kids who are afraid to be part of one."

Elizabeth looked down at her hands.

"Do you want to go back to bouncing around from one foster home to another?"

She didn't. She shook her head.

"You're eleven years old. Unless you're planning to run away, to join a circus, being part of a family is your only viable option."

*The way she said it, it sounded so simple.*

Iron Woman took Elizabeth's chin in her hand. "You won't find a better one."

"I know," she whispered. Her eyes filled again.

"Then say it. Right out loud. 'I want to be part of this family.'"

"I don't know how."

"Then we'll show you. Say it."

*It's true. I do.*

She shivered. "I want to be part of this family."

Iron Woman kissed her forehead very gently.

"I'm awfully glad."

# Chapter Twenty-Four

Elizabeth swallowed the last sip of her tea. It had been hot and sweet and had tasted wonderful.

"Finished?"

Iron Woman carried the cups to the sink and sat down again.

"How to be part of this family, lesson number one. We call each other by name. And it's not Mrs. Sheridan. It's Grandma. Try it."

"Grandma." Elizabeth blushed.

"I like the way that sounds." Iron Woman smiled.

Elizabeth tried to smile back. She wasn't sure how well she succeeded.

"Lesson number two has to do with mistakes. We all make them. In this family, we admit we were wrong and we take our medicine. Then we apologize and do what we can to make amends."

Elizabeth nodded.

"You made a pretty big mistake this morning, didn't you?"

She nodded again.

"What you said to Karen was unfair and unkind."

Elizabeth's ears burned.

"It was also extremely disrespectful."

Elizabeth winced. It had been.

"In this family, that's *never* O.K." She paused. "Understood?"

Elizabeth nodded once more.

"Then it's time to take your medicine." She got up from the table. "The sooner we start, the sooner it's over."

Elizabeth pushed back her chair and followed Grandma up the stairs. Spankings took place in Grandma's bedroom. Elizabeth had never been spanked, and she wondered what it would be like.

As Grandma closed the door, Elizabeth realized that it was the first time she had been inside this room. The only thing that could have been considered at all decorative was the patterned quilt that lay neatly folded over the railing at the foot of the bed.

Elizabeth heard a drawer open. She turned toward the sound and stared. Her own photograph stood among the dozen or so on top of the dresser.

*But . . . ?*

Grandma took a thin wooden paddle from the bottom drawer and nodded toward the bed. Elizabeth swallowed hard and bent over the quilt.

*You get spanked your age. Eleven times.*
"Ready?"

No, she thought. "Yes," she answered.

*Thwap!* She heard the first spank before she felt it. *Thwap!* By the time the third one landed, her backside was on fire. *Thwap! Thwap!* Tears squeezed from between her eyelids. *Thwap! Thwap! Thwap! How many more? Thwap! Thwap! Thwap! Thwap!*

It took her a moment to realize that it was over. She pushed herself to her feet and wiped her eyes with her hands.

"Why don't you go and wash your face?" Grandma slid the dresser drawer closed. "When you're ready, come back down to the kitchen."

Elizabeth slowly made her way to the bathroom. She hadn't imagined being spanked would hurt that much, but if another spanking could erase what she'd said to Karen, she'd ask for it.

As she turned on the tap, Elizabeth wondered how she could possibly face her.

*"There's a drugstore near the amusement park . . ."*

Dozens of Karen's kindnesses, large and small, flickered through her mind. How could she even begin to apologize? She held her fingers under the water and waited for it to get warm.

*Why would Karen want to listen?*

She wondered if Karen still wanted to be her mother. A wave of fear swept from her knees to her neck.

*What if she doesn't?*

The thought immobilized her and she failed to notice an abrupt change in temperature. With a yelp, she pulled her fingers from the steaming water and turned on the cold. She wet a washcloth, rubbed it over her face, and went down the stairs.

Iron Woman—*Grandma*—gave her a quick smile as she came into the kitchen. She had a bag of flour in the crook of one arm, a box of eggs in one hand, and a bottle of vanilla in the other. "That's one hard job over," she said. "For both of us. I do not enjoy spanking my grandchildren."

*"My grandchildren." Me, too.*

Elizabeth felt a terrifying surge of belonging and didn't know what to do with it. Once again, words escaped from her mouth before her brain knew they were there, before she could guard against their release.

"Do you think . . . ?" She faltered.

Midway between refrigerator and table, Grandma stopped and stood still. "That Karen will forgive you?"

Elizabeth held her breath.

"She will." Grandma turned to look directly at her. "Karen understands that people make mistakes." She raised her eyebrows.

Elizabeth couldn't tell whether she was supposed to say something, or if Grandma's expression meant, "That makes sense, doesn't it?"

Nothing made sense. Too many feelings had overcome her this morning without her knowing what they were or why they happened.

Grandma set her things on the table. "Come here," she said gently.

Trembling, Elizabeth stopped just beyond her reach. If she allowed Iron Woman to hug her, the few pieces of herself that she still recognized would come apart. There would be nothing left of the person she knew.

Grandma folded her arms. "Do you hate me?"

Elizabeth's mouth dropped open.

*Because I won't hug her?*

She closed her mouth and shook her head.

"Why not?"

Elizabeth shook her head again.

"I made you stay home. I asked you hard questions and made you cry. I lectured you. I spanked you." She tipped her head to one side. "Why don't you hate me?"

"I don't know," Elizabeth said slowly. "But I don't."

Grandma gave her an encouraging smile. "You're smart. You'll figure it out. And when you do, you'll be as sure as I am about Karen."

Apologies. Grandma had said she could write them. She even offered to deliver them or read them out loud, if Elizabeth wanted her to.

She could not think of anything to say to Karen. "I'm sorry" seemed completely inadequate. She'd given that up for the moment and was trying to write something to the rest of the family. As she had done twenty times, she wrote two or three words and then scribbled them out.

Without any warning, Elizabeth threw up. She was horrified, but could do nothing to stop it. Her stomach lurched a second time, harder. She threw up again, gagged, and started to choke.

"Just let it happen."

Grandma was next to her. Elizabeth vomited once more, the last of her tea. She sat still, breathing hard, feeling flushed and light-headed. After a moment, Grandma handed her a paper towel. Elizabeth wiped her mouth and looked with dismay at the table.

"I'm sorry," she whispered hoarsely. "I didn't mean to."

"Of course you didn't." Grandma's eyes were filled with concern. "Are you all right now?"

"I think so."

Grandma took a brown bottle from the spice cupboard and poured a drop of clear liquid into a drinking glass. "Come and rinse." She filled the glass and set it next to the sink. "A bit of peppermint helps to get rid of the taste," she added, returning the bottle to its shelf. She switched the water to hot and got out a clean dish towel.

The peppermint helped. Elizabeth rinsed her mouth twice. Then she washed her face slowly and felt some of the tension slip out of her shoulders.

"Thank you."

Grandma's brow was still creased. "You're awfully

pale. I think maybe you should lie down for a while. Let's put you on the porch."

Lying down sounded like a wonderful idea. Elizabeth didn't think she would get sick again, but she was terribly tired. Moments later she was stretched out on the cushioned seat of the swing. The screen door banged and Grandma reappeared with a pillow. She tucked it under Elizabeth's head, hesitated for a moment, and then smoothed her hair.

"I'm going to take care of the kitchen, and then I'll be back to check on you." The screen door closed again, gently this time.

It was quiet and shady and green on the porch. A warm, pine-scented breeze blew over her and she slept.

Elizabeth didn't want to wake up, but she couldn't ignore the light any longer. She squirmed and tried to raise one arm. It was caught on something, or under something. Cautiously, she opened her eyes. Blazing sunshine forced her to shut them again.

"Hello."

*Whose voice is that?*

Elizabeth wriggled her arms free of the blanket, shaded her eyes, and reopened them. She knew *where* she was, but she couldn't remember *why*.

"How are you feeling?"

Grandma was sitting in one of the wicker chairs, sewing something. Elizabeth propped herself on one elbow. Her mouth tasted awful and she felt pretty foggy.

"What time is it?" The sun didn't reach the porch until after lunch.

"Quarter to one. You've been asleep for almost three hours."

Buzzing loudly, a large bumblebee darted and hovered across the porch. Elizabeth followed its path until it flew out from under the eaves and disappeared.

"How about some lunch?"

Elizabeth nodded. The only thing she'd had all day was the tea.

Grandma placed her glasses and her sewing on the floor. "I'll fix something. You finish waking up."

They sat in companionable silence. While Elizabeth ate her egg salad sandwich, Grandma hemmed a pair of cutoff jeans. How quickly and surely her hands moved as she stitched. Why had Elizabeth never noticed that before?

"I think I know why you threw up this morning." Grandma snipped a thread and folded the shorts. "And I'm pretty sure it was my fault."

Elizabeth's eyes grew wide.

"After you said you wanted to be part of the family, I didn't give you much chance to get *used* to the notion." She lifted her sewing basket onto her lap. "Most of the time, when a person's got a difficult job to do, it's best to get on with it." She paused. "I wasn't thinking about how it might feel to change your worldview from temporary to permanent."

She gazed out into the yard for several minutes. When she spoke again, her voice was filled with sadness. "You've been pushing people away for *years*, haven't you?"

Their eyes met and Elizabeth quickly looked at the floor. A moment later, she nodded.

"It's going to take some time to reconcile yourself to belonging. I asked you to do too much, too soon, and it got to your tum," Grandma said quietly. "I'm sorry." She looked over her glasses. "Forgive me?"

Elizabeth nodded.

"Good. Then let's leave the letters alone for now."

Elizabeth looked at her hands. This morning seemed a month ago.

"I have an idea." Grandma's eyes began to twinkle. "Do you know how to ride a bike?"

# Chapter
# Twenty-Five

They turned left at the bottom of the driveway and rode into the hot sun at a leisurely pace. Elizabeth was relieved. It had been two years since she'd ridden a bike, and this one was a little big for her. So was the helmet Grandma had insisted she wear. She found her rhythm with the pedals and her mind began to drift.

The morning's events seemed far away, or as though they belonged to someone else. *Nothing* seemed real. Kevin and Karen *couldn't* be keeping her in their family, and she could not *possibly* be going for a bike ride with Iron Woman.

She tried to remember.

They had been getting ready to go to the amusement park. Karen had spoken to her, and she had—

Elizabeth shook her head. She didn't want to think about that part right now.

Grandma had sent her into the house. From the bedroom window, she had watched Kevin put his arm around Karen. She had cried and shaken her head, and Grandma had talked to them both. Finally, Karen had wiped her eyes and nodded. Grandma had given her a hug; then doors had slammed and they all had driven away.

*Then what happened?*

Grandma had called her downstairs. She had made her sit in a chair and she had asked her a lot of questions. Elizabeth couldn't remember what they were. There had been something about Christmas.

*Why?*

Grandma had handed her a book, a bankbook. Her name was in it.

"Elizabeth!"

She looked up. Grandma wasn't in front of her. She pushed the pedals backwards and nothing happened. The bike at the Hartricks' had coaster brakes. This one didn't. She fumbled for the hand brakes and managed to bring the bike to a halt. Grandma was behind her, half a block away. She had turned a corner and Elizabeth had ridden past her without realizing it. Awkwardly, she turned the bike around. She caught up to Grandma and her mind drifted again.

She couldn't recall how it had happened, but she remembered saying, "I want to be part of this family." That had been after she cried. Why had she cried? It was all muted and blurry, with nothing to grab on to.

"This is it!"

Grandma coasted to a stop next to a tall, dense hedge. Wheeling her bike, Elizabeth followed her through a gap in the bushes and up a gravel pathway. It ran between two of the biggest trees Elizabeth had ever seen. It was dark and cool beneath their branches, a sharp and welcome contrast to the burning sunlight.

"We can leave the bikes here." Grandma put down the kickstand and took off her helmet. Elizabeth did the same. Her hair felt sweaty and her bottom ached. Unconsciously, she rubbed it.

"Maybe a bike ride wasn't such a good idea," Grandma observed sympathetically. Elizabeth realized what she was doing and stopped. She shook her head.

"Come and have a look, then," Grandma said. "This place belongs to a friend of mine. She's traveling this summer, and I'm invited to visit whenever I need some solitude."

They crunched their way along the path and up a small, steep hill. Elizabeth could tell from the tang in the air that they were close to the ocean, but she could barely hear the waves. They came to a wooden staircase that was almost vertical and Grandma immediately began to climb. Elizabeth hesitated; then she started after her. She tried not to think about falling backwards, but with each step it grew harder. At last she saw the railing flatten. She heaved herself past the top step and hurried away from the edge.

Fear had kept her from noticing that the sound of waves had grown louder. Now the ocean's thunder assaulted her ears.

"Oh!"

Elizabeth caught her breath and held it.

Below her lay a Japanese garden so perfectly balanced that it looked like a painting. Beyond it, a neatly trimmed lawn sloped toward a stone wall. Beyond that, the ocean crashed onto enormous dark gray boulders, sending white spray dozens of feet into the air. Again and again, the waves roared toward the rocks, as if determined to break past them. Individual drops defied gravity and sparkled and then fell, never the same way twice. The sound was deafening. She stood transfixed, struck with wonder by the sheer power of the water. How could *this* ocean be the one she had seen from the beach?

The wind whipped her hair into and out of her eyes. Elizabeth closed her mouth and tasted salt. She blinked several times and shivered. It was *cold* up here.

She looked to her left. Arms folded against the wind, Grandma was watching her. Elizabeth had always felt uncomfortable being looked at, but just now it was reassuring. She turned back to the waves and stood, spellbound, for a quarter of an hour before Grandma came close enough to speak.

"You're shaking," she hollered over the wind.

"Come this way. I want you to see something, and you can warm up."

To Elizabeth's surprise, she walked toward the ocean. Another gravel path led them through the grass to another wooden staircase. The wind was even stronger here, even louder. Apprehension clutched Elizabeth's throat. The stairs zigzagged below her and she couldn't see where they ended. Grandma waited at the first bend. Elizabeth steeled herself, took the railing in both hands, and started down. As she went around the first corner, the sound of the wind died abruptly and it was suddenly warmer.

They were between the rocks. Giant stones formed a vertical tunnel. They came to the end of the stairs and stepped between two monolithic boulders into another world.

They stood inside an incomplete oval. The farthest rocks were about forty feet away. Through a single space between two of them, Elizabeth could see the blue gray of the ocean. The floor of the enclosure was multileveled, multicolored, and oddly rough in texture. Dozens of pools reflected the sky. Many of them were connected; here and there the rocks were only narrow bridges. It was silent and strange.

*And stunning.*

"It looks like this when the tide is out. When it's in, water covers everything up to there." Grandma pointed to where the smooth rocks met the bumpy ones and then to the little ponds. "Those are tide pools. If you've got sharp eyes . . ."

Elizabeth saw that the rocks were bumpy because they were covered with barnacles. Something darted to her left, a reddish brown crab of some sort. There were living things everywhere. The shapes of the rocks were echoed in the black shells of mussels. Strands of brown kelp twined among them. Some sort of seaweed looked like green hair. Two white birds with long necks had elegant eyebrows. Another bird was smaller and black, with a pointed red beak.

They stepped their way between pools, stopping when Grandma spied something under the water. They saw four kinds of anemones and a purple sea urchin. Grandma called to her happily when she found a small octopus. Elizabeth was too frightened to look, but when she came upon a particularly beautiful whelk, she picked it up.

"May I take some shells . . . home?"

"Not that one." Grandma grinned. "Someone's still using it."

She pointed to where a snail-like creature peeked out of the shell and Elizabeth almost dropped it. None of the shells she'd found on the beach had been occupied. It was one thing, she decided, to collect empty shells. It was another to disturb this place or its inhabitants. She gently put the whelk back where she'd found it.

Grandma had wandered several yards away when

Elizabeth spotted a starfish half in and half out of a pool. Three feet of water separated Elizabeth from the starfish. She took a deep breath and stepped onto the flattest part of the rock. Relief flooded through her; then something broke loose underfoot and she fell.

She landed with an awkward splash and found herself chest deep in water. She looked up, mouth open, eyes wide. She was *in* the ocean! Her heart pounded wildly, but she couldn't feel the rest of her body. She had to get out! She *had* to! But she couldn't move. Her eyes darted every which way.

"Bet that feels good," Grandma said. "I think I'll join you."

She sat down on the edge of the pool, slipped into the water, and waded to where Elizabeth stood paralyzed. "We're lucky it wasn't deeper."

Something in the tone of her voice allowed Elizabeth to realize that her head was, in fact, *above* water. She wasn't dead. And if Grandma was this calm, she probably wasn't going to die. She began to feel the water and found that she could move her arms. Terrified of slipping again, she did not try to move her legs. They began to shake on their own.

"Please," she stammered, "I want to get out."

"O.K." Grandma glanced around the edge of the pool. "Looks like there's a good spot over there." She pointed to a ledge about eight feet away. To Elizabeth, the distance looked like a mile.

"Grab my hand."

Elizabeth did so and held on for life. Grandma took one step, waited for Elizabeth to move, and then waded forward again. They inched their way across the pool.

"Put your hands on that rock and step here. I'm behind you. I'll catch you if you slip." Grandma gave her a quick smile. "Promise."

Elizabeth grasped the rock. Her left sneaker found the foothold and she pulled and pushed at the same time. With a lurch, she was out of the water. Spider-like, she skittered across the rocks and watched puddles form around her hands and knees until Grandma sat down beside her.

"The ride home will be a little uncomfortable, but it felt heavenly to cool off." She twisted the front of her shirt. Water splashed between her feet and snaked down the rock.

Elizabeth pivoted around to sit down. Then she lifted her eyes to the pool. She had been *in* it! And she had survived.

"That's the second big plunge you've taken today." Grandma's voice was gentle. "How are you holding up?"

The words did not register, but Elizabeth sensed that Grandma needed to know if she was O.K. Without taking her eyes from the pool, she nodded.

"You're a brave girl." Grandma squeezed some water from the hem of her shorts and squinted at the sun. "Time to go."

They crossed the rocks together. Elizabeth stepped around and over shells without really seeing them. She had tried to reach the starfish. She had landed on the rock, but she had slipped. She had fallen into the water. She hadn't been able to move. Then Grandma was standing next to her and she could breathe. Grandma had helped her get out of the water.

They were almost to the top of the stairs. Once again, the wind was harsh. Purple goose bumps appeared wherever damp cloth did not cling to skin. Elizabeth was miserably cold, and Grandma had already reached the far stairs, but she could not help herself. She paused at the top of the hill to stare at the crashing water, to marvel again at the height of the spray.

*I was in that water.*

The wind shrieked past her.

*Not those bits of it, but I was in the ocean. I was part of it.*

Getting down the stairs was easier than she anticipated: her fear took second place to her eagerness to reach the sunshine on the other side of the hedge. She also counted each step—with her eyes closed. She didn't open them until she felt gravel slide under her feet.

Earlier, the shade beneath the trees had seemed cool. Now the darkness felt warm and welcoming. Grandma had turned the bicycles around. Elizabeth started to trot down the path; then she slowed to a shuffle. When she reached the bikes, Grandma handed her the oversized helmet. She twisted the strap around one finger. Grandma was poised to push off. If she didn't say it now, she knew she wouldn't. And it needed to be said.

"Grandma?" Elizabeth spoke to the handlebars of her bicycle. "Thank you."

She looked for the briefest moment into her eyes, not long enough to read her expression. Then she untangled the strap and put on the helmet.

"You're welcome," Grandma said. "We'll come again." She turned toward the street. "Next year."

## Chapter
## Twenty-Six

If the ride to the rocks had been leisurely, the ride home was anything but. Elizabeth was forced to keep her wits about her. There were many more cars on the road than there had been earlier, and Grandma seemed to be in a hurry. She was pedaling hard and looked back only once. Elizabeth wondered what she was thinking about and then turned her attention to keeping pace. She was relieved to see the house and vaguely astonished to find it exactly where they had left it.

As they wheeled their bicycles toward the shed, the morning's unfinished business forced itself into her mind. They—everyone, *Karen*—would be home soon. They were probably already in the cars, already driving. The pleasures of the afternoon evaporated and a scratchy wariness took their place.

They left their wet sneakers outside the back door and climbed the steps to the kitchen. Grandma pulled the big pot from its shelf and began to fill it with water.

"If you don't mind, I'll shower first," she said. "Then you can take your time while I work on dinner." She carried the heavy pot to the stove, put on the lid, and turned the burner on low. "If you want it, there's paper on top of the bread box."

The sound of Grandma's bare feet on the wooden stairs was comforting, reassuring somehow. The shower hissed into the tub; then the sound was cut off.

It was dark and peaceful in the kitchen. In the morning sun, the room's bright colors sparkled. Now the blues and reds were shades of gray. Through the window Elizabeth could see the crescent beginnings of late-afternoon shadows. For some reason they struck her as friendly.

Footsteps crossed the floor overhead. A faint rattle came from the stove as the pot began to simmer. How many meals had Grandma cooked in this kitchen? she wondered. How many dishes had she washed?

"Elizabeth?"

She hadn't heard Grandma come down. Standing still in the middle of the kitchen must look pretty odd.

"I was just . . . *listening*."

A flicker of relief skipped into Grandma's eyes and

was immediately replaced by a look of understanding. "It's a good thing to do."

She walked to the sink and put her hand on the wall switch. "I hate to spoil the moment." The light went on. "But we're going to have a bunch of very hungry people to feed." She opened a box of macaroni and poured it into the pot. "I'm guessing they'll be here in about an hour, but everybody always wants to swim before dinner. That gives us a few extra minutes."

She flattened the carton and tossed it into the recycling box. Elizabeth winced.

*Karen's letter . . .*

"The bathroom's all yours. Please put your wet clothes in the mudroom, not in the hamper." Grandma stirred the macaroni, leaning back as a swirl of steam rose toward her. "Someone forgot, and we've got a bunch of mildewed pillowcases."

Elizabeth peeled off her shirt. It was barely damp, but her skin was sticky. She piled her clothes next to the sink and turned on the shower. The sound usually reminded her of rain, but now it made her think of waves against rocks. Ocean noises.

That was it! She suddenly knew how she would apologize to Karen. With a burst of energy, she washed her hair, toweled herself, and headed for the bedroom.

A quick look out the window assured her that the driveway was empty. She climbed into clean clothes, slid her pouch from the pillowcase, and pulled out the cassette. The remains of the label were ragged and uneven, but it couldn't be helped. She took a pen from her dresser, hesitated, and then wrote on the label: *To Karen, From Elizabeth.*

She frowned, wishing she had a ribbon to tie it. She did! Caroline had given her a packet of hair ribbons. It was still there, under her bathing suit. She ripped open the plastic and selected a green one. Carefully, she put the ribbon in one pocket of her shorts and the cassette in the other. She collected her wet clothes from the bathroom and hurried down the stairs.

Grandma glanced at her, and then up at the clock. "That was speedy." She resumed slicing beans.

Elizabeth checked the clock, too. If Grandma had guessed correctly, she had forty-five minutes, but they might be home early for some reason. She'd better hurry. Now that she knew how she was going to apologize to Karen, she thought she could probably write the family a letter as well. She hoped Grandma wouldn't mind too much if she stayed in the kitchen. If she needed to, she wanted to be able to look at her.

She collected paper and pencil and leaned over the table. Not a trace remained of the morning's disaster. She flushed a little at the memory and hoped it hadn't been too awful to clean up.

Grandma paused in her slicing. "I owe Karen an apology, too."

Elizabeth looked up with wide eyes.

"For going into her bag and looking at the bankbook, without her permission." She gave Elizabeth a quick smile. "I think she'll forgive both of us."

Grandma dressed the beans, carried them to the refrigerator, and began to rearrange things on the shelves. Elizabeth watched her until the oven timer rang.

*Get going!*

Slowly, she wrote: *To Karen. I am sorry about what I said.* She twisted the pencil. *I don't know why I said it, but I didn't mean it,* she added, and signed her name. A moment later she wrote, *P.S. I hope you like the tape.*

Satisfied, she took the cassette from her pocket. The paper crackled as she folded it around the plastic, and the package slid around on the table as she tied the ribbon, but at length she succeeded. She printed, *For Karen,* next to the bow and reached for a clean piece of paper.

In fits and starts, she wrote for fifteen minutes. Finally, she put down the pencil and folded the page in quarters. Only when the job was finished did she acknowledge the prickly feeling in her stomach. It had already evolved into queasiness. Nausea and panic were not far away.

Grandma put something into the sink and crossed the room to the table. "Would you like me to give that to Karen?" She tipped her head toward the package.

Elizabeth nodded.

"Would you like me to read this to everyone?" Grandma pointed to the square of paper. "When they get home?"

"Please?" Her voice sounded thick.

Grandma nodded. "Would you like to be some-place else when that happens?" she asked gently.

Elizabeth choked out a breath. *Any* place else. How could she could feel so tired and so tense at the same time?

"I've been debating with myself," said Grandma. "About giving you this." She took an envelope from her pocket. "I want you to have it. I'm not sure this is the moment."

She contemplated Elizabeth.

"You've had a long day. Lots of new experiences, and lots of new feelings. Some of them scary and painful."

She put her elbows on the table, leaned forward, and waited for Elizabeth to meet her gaze. Their eyes locked.

"Not easy, but *worth* it."

*She's giving me a hug.*

Something boiled over. Grandma leapt to take the pan from the burner. Then she gave Elizabeth the envelope and a reassuring smile.

"Take it with you," she said. "Read it when you're ready. Why don't you go back and sit by the barn? It's a good place to listen."

Elizabeth's knees wobbled as she stood up.

"Scoot!" Grandma added. "They'll be home any minute."

Elizabeth scooted.

# Chapter Twenty-Seven

 Elizabeth wanted to sort out the day, but she couldn't stop thinking about Karen. Her shoulders suddenly fell. Kevin and Caroline and Paul must be mad at her, too. She had made Karen cry.

*Are they really going to keep me?*

Grandma had seemed certain of it.

*Grandma. Iron Woman. Mrs. Sheridan.*

How had everything changed? How had this day happened?

She looked down at her untied shoelaces and suddenly thought of Paul's snake. She had wondered how accepting Abby's apology would help Abby. She understood now. Elizabeth hadn't been forced to apologize very often, but whenever she'd had to, she'd only gone through the motions. This time she meant it. That was something else new, something else to sort out.

*Are they really going to keep me?*

*Why would they* want *to?*

*But Iron Woman wouldn't lie . . . would she?*

A car pulled into the driveway and she looked at her watch. Kevin and Karen had arrived less than twenty-four hours ago.

*Do you have to fit in to belong?*

More car doors slammed and Sheridan noise filled the air. The clamor died into a very un-Sheridan quiet that lasted for seventeen minutes. It was broken by a burst of laughter.

*What made them laugh?*

Six minutes later, Petey appeared on the lawn. Somehow, she had known they'd send him to get her. Elizabeth waited where she was, struggling against a desire to hide, even from him.

He stopped an arm's length away and inspected her. "Are you O.K., Turtle?"

*Is he asking because of something his grandmother said or because it's so plain that I'm not?*

She nodded. He took a step forward and quickly kissed her cheek. "That's from Aunt Karen," he said, backing up to look at her again.

Elizabeth closed her eyes. Sunburned and solemn, Petey remained in front of her.

"We have to go back. Mr. Ciminelli is coming."

*The refrigerator man?*

Elizabeth started to laugh, then started to cry, then did both at the same time, and hiccupped to a stop.

*Why not?*

In the last twelve hours, every part of her universe had been turned upside down. Why shouldn't the refrigerator man be part of this day?

Petey gave her a quizzical smile. Then he took her hand and led her across the grass.

They rounded the corner of the house and Grandma came toward them.

"Elizabeth, this is Mr. Ciminelli. He takes our family portraits."

She turned toward the porch. The entire family was there, carefully positioned along the railing.

"Alberto Ciminelli, at your service!" A handsome, plump man kissed Elizabeth's hand. Her eyes became saucers and the porch exploded in laughter.

"Don't worry, Elizabeth," Caroline called. "Mr. C. does that to everyone!"

Mr. Ciminelli released her hand. "Is this pretty girl the last of them, Martha?" His eyes sparkled. "Any little ones in the bushes?"

He pretended to look, sending Sarah into a fit of giggles.

"This is the lot, Alberto." Grandma grinned. "If you find any more, you can take 'em with you. They don't belong to us."

"C'mon up, Elizabeth. You're right here." Kevin

smiled and pointed to a gap in the front row. Karen smiled, too, and her emerald eyes sparkled. Shyly, Elizabeth smiled back.

"And I'm *next* to you," Petey said stoutly.

With astonishingly little fuss, the remaining members of the family assumed their places and Mr. Ciminelli began to issue instructions. He bobbed up and down behind his tripod, peering first over his camera, and then through it. He made a dozen minor adjustments — "this way, a little bit more, good, good." He checked the sky: they'd *just* make the light. He called for smiles, took six pictures, and signaled all clear.

"Dinner's in forty-five minutes," Grandma announced. "If you're going to swim, you'd better hustle." Sheridans, large and small, scurried from sight.

"Four masterpieces, maybe five." Mr. Ciminelli beamed as he folded his tripod.

"Thank you, Alberto," said Grandma. "This one's extra special." She waved as he slammed the trunk of his car.

Elizabeth sat still, numbed as she so often was by Sheridan comings and goings. She would have to find some way to get used to the noise.

"Elizabeth, do you want to come?"

She wasn't sure she could handle yet another new thing, but Karen looked hopeful. She nodded.

"It's about time you christened that bathing suit!" Grandma winked and went into the house.

"Hurry!" said Karen. "Meet you here in five minutes."

Elizabeth's roommates had already changed. "It's so *exciting* when the water's all pink!" Sarah squealed as they trotted past her.

The bathing suit looked smaller than it had in the store. Scissors. She needed scissors to cut off the tags. A pair of nail clippers did the trick and Elizabeth wriggled into the sky blue nylon. It stretched, and she got the straps over her shoulders. Her arms looked funny: fish-belly white at the top, golden brown from the elbows down. She shoved her feet into her sneakers and ran back to the porch. Karen was already there, a towel in each hand.

"Here you go." She handed Elizabeth one of them.

"Thank you."

"C'mon." Karen smiled and pointed to the setting sun. "It's going to be gorgeous."

They walked quickly and caught up to Rachel and Petey.

"We went on twenty *hundred* rides today, Turtle. And I didn't cry. Not even once. Sarah said I would, but I didn't. Right, Mom?"

Rachel ruffled his hair. "Not one speck."

Petey continued his amusement-park monologue until they reached the beach.

*Thank you, Petey.*

They dropped their towels and kicked off their sneakers. Petey dashed ahead. Then he ran back to his mother. "Take me in?"

Rachel smiled. "That's why I came." She swung him onto her hip and waded into the waves.

"Just to our knees?" Karen held out her hand.

Elizabeth quickly discovered that she didn't like the sand at the water's edge. It was damp and gritty and full of sharp bits of shell. Four steps into the water, the sand felt completely different. The valleys between the ripples were smooth and there didn't seem to be any shells. The water was warmer than she expected.

They took three more steps. The sand felt the same, but the water was noticeably cooler. For the first time, Elizabeth felt the rhythm of the waves, pushing and pulling her legs, first toward the beach and then out to sea. She tightened her grip on Karen's fingers.

"Far enough?"

Elizabeth nodded. They stood, hand in hand, feeling the ocean rise and fall and watching the water change color. Kevin chased Paul through the waves. He caught him, threw him into the air, waved to them, and dove after Caroline.

*How can they do that?*

A large surge caught them off guard and Elizabeth was instantly wet to her waist. She was standing *in* the ocean and she was *holding* Karen's hand! She shook her head and Karen looked down in alarm.

"Are you O.K.?"

Elizabeth nodded.

"Look!" Kevin pointed. Just above the horizon, the

sun had spilled sideways. As they watched, it turned crimson and slipped from view.

*Tweet! Tweet! Tweet!* Steve blew his whistle again, Andrew yelled, "Food!" and everyone scrambled out of the water.

Karen and Elizabeth traded hands and waded onto the shore. "I'm just going to get my face wet," Karen said. "I won't be a minute."

The water foamed a little as she ran through it. Elizabeth held her breath as Karen dove. Karen stood up, smoothed the water from her face, and made her way back to the beach.

"All here. Let's go!"

Karen rubbed her hair quickly and threw the towel over her shoulders.

*She would have enjoyed swimming with the others.*

"Thank you."

They reached the road before Karen replied. "Thank *you*, for coming."

Elizabeth sighed. There were so many things she didn't understand.

Dinner's bests consisted of roller coasters and tilt-a-whirls and something called "The Screamer." Listening to the descriptions of hairpin turns and levels of vertigo made Elizabeth glad she hadn't been there.

When Kevin passed her his turn, she could feel Grandma looking at her. "The ocean." She kept her eyes on her plate, but she spoke clearly. "I pass my turn to Paul."

She hadn't been able to decide among the rocks, the tide pools, the beach, and being forgiven. So what she'd said was true. Everyone smiled, and nobody pressed her for details.

Dessert was served and consumed in virtual silence—a happy, sunburned, exhausted silence. There were no arguments from any quarter about the fact that it was time for bed.

Elizabeth gave not one thought to putting on her pajamas. She slid between the sheets and was asleep before she'd pulled her feet in under the blanket.

# Chapter
# Twenty-Eight

"Come on, sleepy. Last call. Rise and shine!"

Grandma rubbed Elizabeth's back for a moment. Then she raised the window shades. Hot yellow sunlight streamed into the room and Elizabeth pulled the pillow over her head.

"Nope!" Grandma tugged it away from her. "They'll be back in twenty minutes, and I promised Karen you'd be ready."

Elizabeth buried her head in the bedspread and Grandma swatted her bottom.

"Up!" she said, firmly. "Put on your bathing suit and come down to the kitchen. You need to eat something." She stood in the doorway until Elizabeth staggered to her feet. Then she gave her a smile and went down the stairs.

Karen had taken Caroline and Paul to get ice cream. They had wanted Elizabeth to go with them, but Karen had decided she needed the rest. Elizabeth ate her sandwich in a fog. When she finished, Grandma lathered her shoulders with sunscreen. She was putting the cap on the bottle when Karen came into the room.

"How are you feeling?" She smiled.

Elizabeth nodded. She was dazed, but alive.

As they walked to the beach, Elizabeth's blood began to make its way to her brain. How was it possible that she was wearing a bathing suit? She vaguely remembered cutting off the tags. How had she been persuaded to do that?

Like fireflies at dusk, bits and pieces of yesterday winked just out of reach.

"Please?" Kevin held out his hand.

In a daydream, Elizabeth took it. They waded into the water.

"Say when."

"When."

Elizabeth warily watched the waves. When she began to tremble, Kevin squeezed her hand. "Time to get out?" he asked gently.

She nodded and they walked back to dry sand.

"Mom was right." Kevin smiled. "You've got a lot of guts."

Paul called to him, and he waved.

"Thank you, Elizabeth." He smiled at her again. Then he splashed his way back into the ocean. Her hand tingled where he had held it.

Elizabeth came down the stairs slowly and paused inside the screen door. The Sheridan uncles were barbecuing, and there was much friendly arguing about sauces and coals. The tribe swarmed happily among fathers, mothers, aunts, uncles, and onto the picnic tables and the porch. Elizabeth didn't exactly want to be by herself, but that level of activity was more than she felt ready to handle. She wandered into the front room and was startled to find Andrew on the sofa with a chessboard.

He asked her if she knew how to play. When she shook her head, he shyly asked if she'd like to learn. She nodded. Andrew grinned and quickly explained the basic rules. They each made ten moves. Elizabeth thought they were still evenly matched until Andrew moved a knight and said, "Check." Two moves later, he smiled gently. "Checkmate."

Elizabeth appreciated the way he'd outflanked her. She smiled back.

"Know what?" He contemplated her. "You're really pretty when you smile."

She stared at him. He blushed and shrugged, looked at her again, and nodded. It was her turn to blush, and she was grateful when Grandma called to them to help carry the food.

Eating on the lawn was easier than eating in the dining room. It was possible to sit next to someone without sitting across from someone else. Elizabeth had the sense, not of being looked at, but that people were making an effort not to look at her. She listened and watched and tried not to think.

Despite having slept until three, Elizabeth was exhausted. When Rachel said it was time for Abby and Sarah to go up to bed, she went with them. In response to a question from Karen, she nodded. She was O.K. She brushed her teeth and climbed into her pajamas. The room suddenly spun.

*Who made my bed?*

She lunged for her pillow. Her fingers grasped a lump beneath the cotton: her pouch was where it belonged. Her shoulders shook uncontrollably and tears poured down her cheeks. Abby watched her for a moment. Then she took Sarah's hand and slipped into the hall.

In less than a minute, Kevin and Karen were at the door.

"Elizabeth?"

The sound of Kevin's voice made her cry harder and she buried her head in the pillow. They sat on the bed, one on each side of her. She couldn't decipher their words, but the tenor of their voices was soothing.

When she woke up the next morning, the bunk bed was empty.

She couldn't remember when Kevin and Karen had left.


Elizabeth stepped onto the sand, her eyes on the water, her mind on the voices nearby. They were familiar but foreign, friendly but alien.

After everyone swam, Andrew suggested a game. They settled on something called crab soccer. Elizabeth was intrigued by the name and watched for several minutes as they scurried across the sand, stomachs skyward, kicking a ball. There was much falling down, much shouting and laughter, and very little score keeping. She shook her head and turned toward the ocean.

Petey had filled a bucket and tipped it over. Now he was dripping wet sand onto the mound. "Hi, Turtle." He looked up. "Want to help?"

Elizabeth sat down across from him. She hated the feeling of the damp sand, but it was fascinating to watch it fall from Petey's fingers onto the spires. He made three more turrets and then urged her to try. She pinched a bit of sloppy sand between her fingertips and moved her hand toward the castle. By the time she reached it, the water was gone and the sand fell in clumps.

*What did I do wrong?*

"You have to go fast." Petey demonstrated.

She tried again with greater success, and he beamed encouragement at her. They took turns and the mound grew taller. When Elizabeth added a large drip to one side, a turret collapsed and a third of the castle fell down. She looked up in alarm.

Petey was laughing. "That *always* happens, Turtle!" His cobalt eyes danced.

They started again. When the others went back into the water, Petey crawled over to sit next to her. He shoveled sand into the bucket.

"Are you O.K. now?" He stopped shoveling. "For real?"

Elizabeth's throat was instantly full.

*How can I possibly answer that question? I don't know how O.K. feels.*

"I think so," she finally said. "Are you?"

Petey looked directly at her and nodded. She closed her eyes and tears slid down her cheeks.

*How could I have tried to unmatter you?*

Petey dripped sand onto the back of her hand. When she opened her eyes, he smiled.

"How are you doing?" Karen asked as they walked back from the beach.

*Doing?*

Elizabeth squinted up at her.

"Sheridan uproar takes a lot of getting used to." Karen rolled her eyes and grinned. "I remember feeling as though my head would burst!"

Karen *had felt that way?*

Elizabeth gave her an astonished and grateful smile.


Elizabeth and Caroline had finished setting the tables and were sitting together on the sofa. The sunlight played tag with the shadows on the floor, occasionally dancing up the fireplace. It was the first time Elizabeth had really noticed the front room.

"It's *pretty* in here!"

"Wait'll you see it at Christmas!"

They sat in silence for several minutes.

"Why are you crying?" Caroline asked quietly.

Elizabeth hadn't been aware that she was. She rubbed her wet cheeks. "I don't know," she said simply.

Caroline peered at her with concern. "Want me to get Mom?"

Elizabeth shook her head and managed to smile. The lines disappeared from Caroline's forehead and she smiled back.


"I'm sorry about last night."

Elizabeth glanced at Abby and Sarah. Then she concentrated on buttoning her pajamas.

"That's O.K.," Abby said quickly. "It was kind of fun to sleep on the couch."

Elizabeth's eyes filled with tears.

"Really, Elizabeth," Abby insisted. "You didn't do it on purpose. It's not like you put a snake . . ." Her voice trailed off as she realized what she'd said.

Sarah looked back and forth between them. Her eyebrows had climbed up under her bangs and Elizabeth suddenly started to giggle. Abby and Sarah stared, openmouthed, and Elizabeth's giggle turned into a chuckle.

When Paul called, "What's so funny?" from the doorway, the three of them were laughing too hard to give him an answer.

# Chapter
## Twenty-Nine

After breakfast, the grown-ups disappeared: the women to the second floor, and the men out of doors. As Elizabeth swept the last of the pine needles from the steps, Elena and Rachel came onto the porch wearing dresses. A moment later, Karen and Grandma followed them out.

Elizabeth blinked. She had seen Karen in a dress, but she'd never seen Grandma in anything but shorts or a bathing suit. She was wearing earrings and lipstick. Her dress was a subtle mosaic of blues, and a navy purse was tucked under one arm. She looked oddly delicate and a bit uncertain.

"Hold it, hold it!"

Steve came around the side of the house waving a

camera. All four women groaned but arranged themselves on the stairs and smiled when he asked. His
brothers and he wished them a wonderful day, and
the women drove off.

Adam appeared at the door and his father asked
him to assemble the troops. He grinned and saluted.
Within minutes, the porch was full. Tim read the job
list and called for volunteers to trim bushes, wax
floors, repair the porch steps, clean the stove and the
refrigerators, wash windows, pull weeds, and paint
the mudroom.

Molly volunteered to paint and astonished
Elizabeth by asking if she wanted to help. Dumbly,
she nodded. Tim took Petey to buy supplies, and
Kevin challenged them to see how much they could
accomplish by eleven thirty. Steve hollered "Charge!"
and everyone scattered.

Elizabeth and Molly moved the clothes baskets
to the hall and emptied and washed the shelves. Together, being careful not to disconnect any pipes, they
wrestled the washer and dryer away from the wall.

"Eeeeww!" Molly wrinkled her nose. "Talk about
*disgusting.*"

Elizabeth nodded sympathetically and offered to
get the broom. They swept an enormous pile of lint
from the backs of the machines and washed the walls.
The back door banged as Molly dropped her sponge
into the bucket.

"Perfect timing, Uncle Tim."

He groaned as he lowered four gallons of paint onto the linoleum. "Should've made two trips."

"Can I paint?" Petey was holding a paper bag full of brushes and fuzzy pink rollers. His father smiled at Molly and Elizabeth and then down at Petey.

"I was hoping you'd help me trim bushes," he said. "You're old enough to use the red clippers, don't you think?" Petey's face lit up.

"'Bye, Molly! 'Bye, Turtle!" He pulled his father toward the door.

"Uncle Tim's as tactful as they come. Have you ever painted?"

Elizabeth shook her head. Molly showed her how to load the roller. Then she suggested Elizabeth start by painting the edges of the walls with a brush. After a while, they would trade. Molly had finished one-sixth of the ceiling when her father called her. She frowned and set the roller into the tray.

"Be right back."

Elizabeth nodded and continued to paint. She found that she really enjoyed it. There was a trick to putting the right amount of paint on the brush, but it was extremely satisfying to cover the dingy yellow with sparkling white. She finished the edge between the plaster wall and the wooden panels, painted around the door frame, and then borrowed the chair Molly had been using and painted the corners where

the walls met the ceiling. The room looked outlined,
like a coloring book.

Elizabeth wondered where Molly had gone. The
smell of the paint had gotten stuck in her throat and
she decided she was thirsty. As she opened the little
refrigerator, she thought of Mr. Ciminelli.

*Wasn't the picture . . . ?*

She took a can from a very clean shelf, closed the
door, and looked at the calendar. The family portrait
had been scheduled for Friday. Tomorrow.

She carried her pop back to the mudroom, set
it on the dryer, and picked up the roller. It hadn't
looked *that* hard.

It hadn't *looked* it, but it *was.* It was difficult to
coat the roller evenly; the edges dripped and paint
splattered onto her arms. She had to keep getting
down from the chair to get more paint, and when she
glanced up, it all looked blotchy. The room was
small, but by the time she finished the ceiling every
part of her ached.

She sat down on the floor to finish her pop. The
back door banged and Kevin stepped into the room.

"Wow," he said with approval. "Nice work,
Elizabeth." She followed his gaze. The part that had
started to dry looked pretty good.

"I hope that stuff's water based." Kevin grinned.

Elizabeth looked down. White paint covered her
hands and her arms. Two drips snaked down one leg,

and there was a patch of white on the other where she'd bumped the roller.

"Molly sends her apologies. She didn't abandon you. We had to ask her to supervise Sarah and Paul." He smiled again. "Ready for a swim? You've earned it."

"If it's O.K.," she stammered, "I'd rather keep going."

So far, the roller had commanded her full attention. Now that she had gotten the hang of it, Elizabeth wanted time by herself. It was the first time since Monday she'd felt *able* to think.

Kevin looked disappointed and doubtful. "You sure?" She nodded. "All right. We'll call you for lunch."

Painting walls was much easier than painting ceilings. Her mind drifted. It was next to impossible that Mr. Ciminelli had changed the appointment. Why had the Sheridans done it? Why had *anything* happened the way that it had?

*Grandma.*

Elizabeth pictured Grandma dressed up on the porch and decided she preferred the way she usually looked—like herself, the way she looked in the kitchen. She caught her breath and slowly put the roller into the pan.

*Where's Grandma's letter?*

She hadn't read it, and she couldn't remember having put it away anywhere. She wiped her hands on a rag and dug through the load of dark clothes. There were the shorts she had worn. Both pockets were empty.

Elizabeth ran up the stairs, stood next to her bed, and tried to remember. She had fallen asleep in her clothes. Grandma must have made her bed. She would have taken laundry down, and she always checked pockets. Where would she have put it? Elizabeth opened the top drawer of her dresser. The letter was there.

She took two pieces of paper from the envelope: one white, the other crisp and yellow with age. The top one was penned in Grandma's neat script.

*Dear Elizabeth,*

*Sorting out what it means to be part of this family will be a big job. I thought this letter might help.*

*Grandma*

Elizabeth unfolded the second piece of paper. The ink was faded and purple, but the handwriting was clear.

*Dear Martha,*

*It's seventy-two hours before your wedding, and if you weren't nervous, you wouldn't be human. Eddie is* <u>hopelessly</u> *in love with you—and he's a wreck!*

*But apart from the usual prenuptial jitters, it occurs to me that you might be apprehensive about annexing yourself to the Sheridan clan.*

*There are a <u>lot</u> of us! We're loud, and we tease, and we never stop talking. More than once I've suspected you've felt overwhelmed, and I wanted you to know how very, <u>very</u> glad we all are that you are joining the family.*

*Your (almost!) mother-in-law*

She reread each page. Then she tucked the envelope into her pillowcase. She smoothed the bedspread, walked back down to the mudroom, and loaded the roller. She didn't start to cry until she'd finished painting one wall. She didn't stop until the last of the yellow had been covered with white.

In the middle of the third wall, Molly came to call her for lunch. She took one look at Elizabeth and went to get Kevin. He watched her for several minutes from the doorway and left. He returned a moment later and set a sandwich and a glass of iced tea on the washing machine.

"You're doing a terrific job," he said quietly, and disappeared.

He came back at three. Elizabeth had covered two sets of olive green panels with Wedgewood blue, including the awkward one behind the washer and dryer, and had begun the third side.

Kevin gave her a small smile. "You'd rather finish than swim."

She nodded. He crossed the room, kissed the top of her head, and went out the back door.

"Look over *here!*"

The tribe was giving Grandma a tour of the outdoor improvements. There were four feet of paneling left to paint, and Elizabeth was relieved when the voices faded toward the front of the house. Just as she finished, Kevin and Karen and Grandma came down the steps from the kitchen. Wet paintbrush in hand, she looked up.

"Heavens, what a difference!" Grandma exclaimed. "It's *beautiful.*" She beamed as she looked around the room and then at Elizabeth. "You did all of this?"

"Molly helped."

Kevin shook his head. "Only for an hour. Then we needed her outside."

"You're something else, Elizabeth. Thank you." Grandma smiled. "*Very* much."

A flash of light filled the room. Elizabeth dropped the paintbrush and blinked in confusion.

"Kevin!" Karen said sharply.

He blushed and then grinned. Karen started to laugh. Grandma made a wry face at Kevin and joined Karen in laughter.

"Sorry. Couldn't resist." Kevin held up the camera. "Blackmail material, Elizabeth. If you ever break curfew, I'll show this to your boyfriend!"

*Blackmail? Curfew?*

"He's teasing, Elizabeth." Karen opened her purse and took out a small mirror. "See?"

Her face was spattered and streaked with white

and blue paint. She wouldn't have to worry about the picture: she was unrecognizable. She started to smile and felt the paint pull at her cheeks.

"Let me get changed," Grandma said, "and I'll help you get some of that off."

Grandma set down a steaming bucket of water and a gallon-sized jug of vinegar. Her earrings were gone, she had on her gray shorts, and her feet were bare.

"This stinks, but it's better than ammonia." She tipped the jug into the water. "Soak your hands while I start on your face." Grandma dipped a washcloth into the water and rubbed one cheek.

*Like the cotton candy and Petey . . .*

"Close your eyes." Grandma massaged the bridge of her nose with the warm washcloth. Then she moved it across her eyelid. "Your eyelashes are blue!"

Elizabeth blinked. Grandma rinsed the washcloth and smiled.

"Close." She repeated the process on the other side.

"Let's see those hands." Elizabeth lifted them out of the water. They were better, but not by a lot. "Keep soaking," Grandma grunted as she got to her feet. She came back with a nailbrush. "Try this." It worked, although it seemed to Elizabeth that paint and skin came off in equal amounts.

Ten minutes later, Grandma raised one eyebrow and sat back on her heels. "I'm not sure we've improved things, and you smell like a pickle." She grinned. "Let's try a shower."

Elizabeth closed the bathroom door, looked into the mirror, and gasped. There was at least a quart of paint in her hair and her face was a ghoulish gray. Quickly, she turned on the water.

They were eating dessert.

"You smell funny, Grandma." Petey squinted.

"You, too, Turtle."

Grandma sat up very tall and looked down her nose. "Our taste in perfume is apparently unappreciated," she said to Elizabeth in an elegant voice. There were giggles all around them. Grandma leaned toward her and whispered loudly. "I guess we'd better go swimming!"

Elizabeth smiled back as the room exploded in laughter and cheers.

It was a picture-perfect evening for a swim.

When they got home, they gathered in the front room and took turns telling stories. Elizabeth became aware of how exhausted she was and let her mind wander. She sat up suddenly. Tim was speaking, and she knew what he was going to say next.

*She robbed 'em blind!*

"She robbed 'em blind!" he finished. And as she had known they would, everyone laughed. She hadn't understood the joke, but she had known how it ended! Something pleasant glowed in her chest.

The day's labors overcame her again and she was relieved when bedtime arrived. Out of habit, she felt

for her pouch and was momentarily surprised to feel
something beneath it. Then, for what seemed the
thousandth time this week, her eyes filled with tears.

She fell asleep wondering why being part of a
family seemed to mean crying a lot.

# Chapter
# Thirty

The kitchen looked unfamiliar without Grandma in it.

Elizabeth had slept until nine. Downstairs, she learned that Steve, Kevin, and Tim had taken their mother out to breakfast. Elena, Rachel, and Karen were already wearing the whistles. Elizabeth hurried to change and felt frustrated when her body worked against her. All her muscles were tight and sore. As they walked, she decided there were two reasons she ached: painting, and the fact that it was the last day.

When they reached the sand, she surveyed the beach. Her eyes came to rest on her rock and she stared at it until the sound of the whistle broke her concentration. Everyone scurried out of the water and stood together, dripping and laughing, while the waves continued to rush up behind them. Caroline waved to her. She waved back.

*I wish Kevin and Grandma were here.*

Elizabeth was astonished at having had the thought, but once it was in her mind, it refused to budge. When they finally crossed the sand, she was ridiculously relieved to see them both.

*"Do you hate me?"*

When Grandma had asked her that question, Elizabeth had been surprised to find that she didn't. As she watched her carry Petey into the water, she realized that she was no longer afraid of her.

*When did I stop being frightened? And why?*

She didn't know, and she couldn't remember why she had spent so much of the summer trying to avoid her. For the rest of the day, she watched her and thought.

After dinner, she took a jelly jar out of the recycling box and ripped two paper towels from the roll. Upstairs, she tucked her pouch into her pocket and slipped a blue hair ribbon from the package in her top drawer. She collected paper and pencil, went into the bathroom, and locked the door.

She took four shells from the pouch, carefully wrapped them in one of the paper towels, and put them into the jar. *Dear Petey*, she wrote. *These are the shells I was thinking about when I didn't hear Caroline's question. I want you to have them. Elizabeth.* She folded the note, put it on top of the paper towel, and firmly tightened the lid.

Quickly, she opened the square plastic box and plucked the sand dollar from between the sponges. She wrapped it in the second paper towel and tied it with the ribbon. She wrote five words, folded the paper, and tucked it under the bow.

The jar and the sand dollar she put into her top drawer. Grandma's letter went into her pouch, and the pouch into her suitcase. Slowly, she walked down the stairs and out onto the lawn.

The night was windless and warm. The moon had risen and insects hummed all around her. The adults were talking quietly on the porch, the younger kids were listening to Caroline read, and the older kids were playing a game in the front room. Elizabeth stood still, cautiously tasting tranquility.

The screen door closed without banging. Adam paused briefly before coming down the steps. "Feel like taking a walk?" He glanced toward the porch. "They said we could go down to the beach."

Elizabeth hesitated. Then she nodded. Adam hadn't spoken to her all week. She'd been aware that he had been watching her, but he'd kept his distance.

She had watched Adam, too. Since his parents arrived, he'd seemed more relaxed, more like a kid. He had cheerfully relinquished his beach whistle to his father and the barbecue to his uncles. He had teased his aunts, played board games to win, and wrestled with Andrew and Paul.

They watched the water for almost ten minutes before Adam spoke.

"Grandma thinks we've got potential as friends." He glanced at her and then looked straight ahead. "She says we have at least three things in common: we're stubborn, we're smart, and we're shy."

Elizabeth stared at him.

"It's true." He shrugged. "I hardly ever say anything in school, and I've never had the nerve to ask a girl out." He picked up a shell and turned it over several times. "That's one of the reasons I like spending time with my family. I don't have to pretend or perform."

The water glittered silvery gray in the moonlight, and the sand was colorless. A small dark creature scurried along the water's edge. Finally, Adam put down the shell, hugged his knees to his chest, and spoke to his sneakers.

"I adore my family, Elizabeth. Every person in it, and the times we're together most of all." He took an irregular breath. "I couldn't understand how anyone could not want to be part of it."

The waves crashed softly.

"When Mom and Dad told us Uncle Kevin and Aunt Karen were adopting, you know what's the first thing I thought?" He looked at her and then at the water. "What a *lucky* kid."

Elizabeth swallowed hard.

"I couldn't wait to meet you." He snorted a painful little laugh. "And I've been *mad* at you since you arrived. Because you wouldn't do anything with the rest of us. Because you weren't making any effort to be a sister or a cousin. Because you hurt people's feelings. Because our family's so *special*, and you didn't see it."

He crossed his legs and began to comb the sand with his fingers. "At least, it didn't seem like you did. I've been trying to imagine what it's like to be you." He side-armed a shell toward the water. "And I *can't*." He threw another shell. "Belonging to my family is so much a part of who I am that I don't have any way to *begin* to understand what your life's been like."

Elizabeth felt as though she should say something, but she didn't know what. "I don't know what it's like to be you," she finally offered. "I don't know how it feels to belong."

Adam stretched his legs out in front of him. "You really didn't believe you'd be with Uncle Kevin and Aunt Karen for always?"

She shook her head and looked down. "I had no reason to expect it."

"Do you believe it now?"

Her eyes filled with tears. "I'm trying to."

They sat in silence for a long time before Adam flopped onto his stomach and propped himself on his elbows.

"One summer, my parents had to go somewhere

for a few days. The others hadn't gotten here yet, so we were here with Uncle Kevin and Aunt Karen and Grandma. I was eight, Caroline was six, and Molly was four. Paul was just starting to walk."

Picturing Paul as a toddler made it easier for Elizabeth to imagine Adam at eight.

"Grandma and Aunt Karen had gone to get groceries, and Uncle Kevin was watching us. I begged to go swimming, but he said we had to wait until Paul woke up from his nap. He asked me to find something to do for an hour and started playing with Caro and Molly."

A warm-cool breeze blew over them, briefly masking the sound of the waves.

"I was bored and impatient, so I decided to go swimming by myself. I knew I wasn't supposed to, that I was breaking a rule, but I was too little to *really* understand the danger." He paused. "Or how frightened Uncle Kevin would be if he didn't know where I was."

Elizabeth's heart skipped a beat.

*Like the Fourth of July . . .*

"When Aunt Karen and Grandma got home, Uncle Kevin realized I wasn't there. I was standing in the water when he came running across the sand. He stopped as soon as he saw me, and his face turned white. Then he walked into the water, in his clothes and his sneakers, and dragged me all the way home by my wrist. He didn't say a single word until we got to the porch. Then he told me he was too angry to talk to me, too angry to do *anything,* and that I should sit on the swing until he said I could move."

Elizabeth tried to picture Kevin that angry, and couldn't.

"Pretty soon everyone went down to the beach. Uncle Kevin didn't even look at me when they left. I had never seen him that angry. I hadn't known he *could* be that angry, and I was really, really frightened. It didn't take me very long to convince myself that he didn't want to be my uncle anymore."

Elizabeth shivered.

"It was probably only twenty minutes before he came back, but it felt like a week. He sat down next to me and explained why he'd been so upset, but I could hardly listen to what he was saying. Finally, I blurted it out. I asked him if he still wanted to be my uncle. He said that I'd made a mistake, but nothing I ever did, no matter *how* horrible, could make him not want to be my uncle."

Elizabeth thought Adam had finished, but he took a deep breath and continued in a soft voice. "I started to cry, and he hugged me for a really long time."

He squinted at the water. "Then Aunt Karen started shouting to him from the driveway. Caroline had cut her foot on a shell. She needed stitches and they took her to the hospital."

Adam returned his gaze to the sand. "When they got back, I was standing on the porch. Caroline's foot was all bandaged and Uncle Kevin carried her into the house. Then he came out and said, 'Where were we?' and hugged me again." He twisted a strand of seaweed between his fingers. Then he looked up at her. "Does that help?" he asked quietly.

She nodded. It *had* helped her. To understand Adam as much as Kevin. They watched the waves for a while.

"Can I ask you something?" Adam said lightly.

Elizabeth nodded.

"How did you know about my bet with Andrew?"

"I heard you through the window."

Adam looked down. Elizabeth thought he might be blushing, but it was impossible to tell in this light.

"When Grandma got to the end of your letter, I almost fell off the porch."

Elizabeth had forgotten that she had written, *P.S.: Adam owes Andrew five dollars*, at the bottom of the page.

"No one understood until Andrew explained about the bet. Then Grandma said, 'Elizabeth got spanked this morning, Adam. You'll have to pay up!' and everyone laughed."

*That's what had been funny.*

Elizabeth smiled at him briefly. Then she looked at the sand.

"Can I ask *you* something?"

"Sure."

"Did Grandma make you bring me down here?"

He chuckled and shook his head. "She merely reminded me we're leaving tomorrow." He looked up and she followed his gaze. The moon was almost overhead. "It's late. We'd better get back."

They walked in silence until they reached the driveway.

"Adam?"

He stopped and turned toward her.

"I'm sorry I ruined your summer."

"You didn't," he said quietly. "It hasn't been the summer I expected it to be. But I'll say it again, and I mean it." He gave her a Sheridan smile. "Welcome to the family."

V. M. CALDWELL taught science for fifteen years. She has also been a chef, printing press operator, paste-up artist, silk screen photographer, switchboard operator, and farmhand, and has participated in a Minnesota Outward Bound experience. She has two sons, both of whom were adopted. This is her debut book.

*Gildaen, The Heroic Adventures of a Most Unusual Rabbit*
by Emilie Buchwald
*Chicago Tribune* Book Festival Award,
Best Book for Ages 9-12

Gildaen is befriended by a mysterious being who has lost his
memory but not the ability to change shape at will. Together
they accept the perilous task of thwarting the evil sorcerer,
Grimald, in this tale of magic, villainy, and heroism.

*No Place*
by Kay Haugaard

Arturo Morales and his fellow sixth-grade classmates decide to
improve their neighborhood and their lives by building a park
in their otherwise concrete, inner-city Los Angeles barrio.
The kids are challenged by their teachers to figure out what
it would take to transform the neighborhood junkyard in to a
clean, safe place for children to play. Despite their parents'
skepticism and the threat of street gangs, Arturo and his classmates struggle to prove that the actions of individuals—even
kids—can make a difference.

*The Gumma Wars*
by David Haynes

Larry "Lu" Underwood and his fellow West 7th Wildcats have
been looking forward to Tony Rodriguez's birthday fiesta all
year—only to discover that Lu must also spend the day with
his two feuding "gummas," the name he gave his grandmothers
when he was just learning to talk. The two "gummas," Gumma
Jackson and Gumma Underwood, are hostile to one another,
especially when it comes to claiming the affection of their only
grandson. On the action-packed day of Tony's birthday, Lu,
a friend, and the gummas find themselves exploring the sights
of Minneapolis and St. Paul—and eventually find themselves
enjoying each other's company.

*Business As Usual*
by David Haynes

In Mr. Harrison's sixth-grade class, the West 7th Wildcats
must learn how to run a business. Kevin Olsen, one of the
Wildcats as well as the class clown, is forced out of the
Wildcat group and into an unwilling alliance working in
a group with the Wildcats' nemesis, Jenny Pederson. In
the process of making staggering amounts of cookies for
Marketplace Day, the classmates venture into the realm of
free enterprise, discovering more than they imagined about
business, the world, and themselves.

*The Monkey Thief*
by Aileen Kilgore Henderson
New York Public Library Best Books of the Year:
"Books for the Teen Age"

Twelve-year-old Steve Hanson is sent to Costa Rica for eight months to live with his uncle. There he discovers a world completely unlike anything he can see from the cushions of his couch back home, a world filled with giant trees and insects, mysterious sounds, and the constant companionship of monkeys swinging in the branches overhead. When Steve hatches a plan to capture a monkey for himself, his quest for a pet leads him into dangerous territory. It takes all of Steve's survival skills—and the help of his new friends—to get him out of trouble.

*The Summer of the Bonepile Monster*
by Aileen Kilgore Henderson
Milkweed Prize for Children's Literature
Alabama Library Association
1996 Juvenile/Young Adult Award

Eleven-year-old Hollis Orr has been sent to spend the summer with Grancy, his father's grandmother, in rural Dolliver, Alabama, while his parents "work things out." As summer begins, Hollis encounters a road called Bonepile Hollow, barred by a gate and a real skull and bones mounted on a board. "Things that go down that road don't ever come back," he is told. Thus begins the mystery that plunges Hollis into real danger.

### Treasure of Panther Peak
by Aileen Kilgore Henderson

Twelve-year-old Page Williams begrudgingly accompanies her mother, Ellie, as she flees her abusive husband, Page's father. Together they settle in a fantastic new world—Big Bend National Park, Texas. Wild animals stalk through the park, and the nearby Ghost Mountains are filled with legends of lost treasures. As Page tests her limits by sneaking into forbidden canyons, Ellie struggles to win the trust of other parents. Only through their newfound courage are they able to discover a treasure beyond what they could have imagined.

### I Am Lavina Cumming
by Susan Lowell
Mountains & Plains Booksellers Association Award

In 1905, ten-year-old Lavina is sent from her home on the Bosque Ranch in Arizona Territory to live with her aunt in the city of Santa Cruz, California. Armed with the Cumming family motto, "Courage," Lavina deals with a new school, homesickness, a very spoiled cousin, an earthquake, and a big decision about her future.

### The Boy with Paper Wings
by Susan Lowell

Confined to bed with a viral fever, eleven-year-old Paul sails a paper airplane into his closet and propels himself into mysterious and dangerous realms in this exciting and fantastical adventure. Paul finds himself trapped in the military diorama on his closet floor, out to stop the evil commander, KRON. Armed only with paper and the knowledge of how to fold it, Paul uses his imagination and courage to find his way out of dilemmas and disasters.

*The Secret of the Ruby Ring*
by Yvonne MacGrory
Winner of Ireland's Bisto "Book of the Year" Award

Lucy gets a very special birthday present, a star ruby ring, from her grandmother and finds herself transported to Langley Castle in the Ireland of 1885. At first, she is intrigued by castle life, in which she is the lowliest servant, until she loses the ruby ring and her only way home.

A *Bride for Anna's Papa*
by Isabel R. Marvin
Milkweed Prize for Children's Literature

Life on Minnesota's iron range in 1907 is not easy for thirteen-year-old Anna Kallio. Her mother's death has left Anna to take care of the house, her young brother, and her father, a black-smith in the dangerous iron mines. So she and her brother plot to find their father a new wife, even attempting to arrange a match with one of the "mail order" brides arriving from Finland.

*Minnie*
by Annie M. G. Schmidt
Winner of the Netherlands' Silver Pencil Prize
as One of the Best Books of the Year

Miss Minnie is a cat. Or rather, she *was* a cat. She is now a human, and she's not at all happy to be one. As Minnie tries to find and reverse the cause of her transformation, she brings her reporter friend, Mr. Tibbs, news from the cats' gossip hotline—including revealing information that one of the town's most prominent citizens is not the animal lover he appears to be.

*The Dog with Golden Eyes*
by Frances Wilbur
Milkweed Prize for Children's Literature

Many girls dream of owning a dog of their own, but Cassie's wish for one takes an unexpected turn in this contemporary tale of friendship and growing up. Thirteen-year-old Cassie is lonely, bored, and feeling friendless when a large, beautiful dog appears one day in her suburban backyard. Cassie wants to adopt the dog, but as she learns more about him, she realizes that she is, in fact, caring for a full-grown Arctic wolf. As she attempts to protect the wolf from urban dangers, Cassie discovers that she possesses strengths and resources she never imagined.

*Behind the Bedroom Wall*
by Laura E. Williams
Milkweed Prize for Children's Literature
New York Public Library Best Books of the Year:
"Books for the Teen Age"

It is 1942. Thirteen-year-old Korinna Rehme is an active member of her local *Jungmädel*, a Nazi youth group, along with many of her friends. Korinna's parents, however, secretly are members of an underground group providing a means of escape to the Jews of their city and are, in fact, hiding a refugee family behind the wall of Korinna's bedroom. As Korinna comes to know the family, and their young daughter, her sympathies begin to turn. But when someone tips off the Gestapo, loyalties are put to the test and Korinna must decide in what she believes and whom she trusts.

*The Spider's Web*
by Laura E. Williams

Thirteen-year-old Lexi Jordan has just joined The Pack, a group of neo-Nazi skinheads, as a substitute for the family she wishes she had. After she and The Pack spray paint a synagogue, Lexi hides from her pursuers on the front porch of elderly Ursula Zeidler, a former member of the Hitler Youth Group, who painfully recalls her ugly anti-Semitic Nazi activities and betrayal of a friend, actions she now bitterly rues. When her younger sister becomes enthralled with Lexi's new "family," Lexi realizes the true meaning of The Pack and has little time to save herself and her sister from its sinister grip.

Milkweed Editions publishes with the intention of making a humane impact on society, in the belief that literature is a transformative art uniquely able to convey the essential experiences of the human heart and spirit.

To that end, Milkweed publishes distinctive voices of literary merit in handsomely designed, visually dynamic books, exploring the ethical, cultural, and esthetic issues that free societies need continually to address.

Milkweed Editions is a not-for-profit press.

Interior design by Elizabeth Cleveland
Typeset in Electra
by Stanton Publication Services, Inc.
Printed on acid-free 55# Sebago Antique Cream paper
by Maple-Vail Book Manufacturing